MW01169969

CHRISTMAS HORROR

Vol. 3

DRP

PUBLISHED BY
DARK REGIONS PRESS, LLC.
—2020—

CHRISTMAS HORROR VOLUME 3
Copyright © 2020 Dark Regions Press

This is a work of fiction. All characters, events or organizations in it are products of the author's imaginations or used fictitiously.

All rights reserved.

Making Merry @ 2020 by Simon Strantzas
All I Want For Christmas Is Your Two Front Teeth @ 2020 by Jeff Strand
Sugar, Spice, and Everything Nice @ 2020 by Stephanie M. Wytovich
Christmas in July @ 2020 by John Palisano
The Ever Green @ 2020 by James Chambers
Welcome to the Party, Pal @ 2020 by William Meikle
ChristMassacre™: The Last Christmas @ 2020 by Jason V Brock
Chrysalis @ 2020 by Richard Thomas
The Best Cookie Dough Ever @ 2020 by Lisa Morton
The Season of Giving @ 2020 by Richard Chizmar and Norman Partridge

A Note from Santa @ 2020 by William F. Nolan
Little Warriors @ 2020 by Gene O'Neill
I Saw Santa @ 2020 by Steve Rasnic Tem
Silent Night @ 2020 by Richard Chizmar
December Birthday @ 2020 by Jeff Strand

Dark Regions Press, LLC
500 Westover Drive Unit 12565
Sanford, NC 27330
DarkRegions.com

Edited by Chris Morey
Cover Design, Cover Art, Interior Art, © 2020 by Zach McCain

ISBN: 978-1-62641-299-6

VOL 3

CHRISTMAS HORROR

TABLE OF CONTENTS

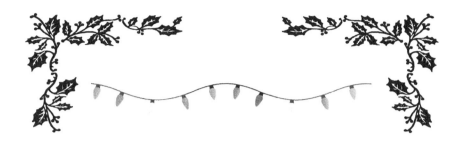

MAKING MERRY

Simon Strantzas

lack shiny boots scrape the inside of the chimney. Ash like clouds of smoke around him as he descends, but the excitement of what he'll find at the bottom, of the faces of the good children as they open their gifts, is buoyant enough, fills him with the seasonal spirit. It rushes into his face with the blood, the two casting a rosy haze across his cheeks.

Nicholas lands at the foot of the chimney, in the damp embers of a cold fireplace, and, heavy green sack over shoulder, steps into the room. Immediately, he knows something is wrong. There is no tree. No stockings, hung with care. There is no mistletoe or tinsel or candy shaped like canes. There are no cookies, no milk; no scrambling, pattering feet. There is nothing but cold, and the sound of cloven hooves waiting for him above.

He is covered in ash, and though the scarlet of his winter's garb still beams from beneath, the smudges and soot rob him of his splendor. And for Nicholas, the splendor is what's important. So much so he doesn't think to pat himself off, his chubby hands working by memory. He cautiously steps further into the room. It's dark and damp and smells as though it has never been occupied. And, yet, he has come, he has been summoned as they all summon him, all the good children in all the houses in all the world. He has been summoned to offer reward in the shape of small boxes wrapped in paper, the contents of which are all a child could want. He is an agent of order, of karma. He is the great arbiter. The final judge of those who deserve, and those who do not. His greatest gift is that of the season's splendor, bestowed upon the worthy, while the rest are left to weep over what they shall ever be denied.

And, yet, in that tiny dank home into which he has been summoned he can find no one. But if there is no child radiating goodness, how then has he been called? Nicholas consults his list, uncertain how the mistake could have occurred, confused how a nameless entry could be in the final tally. It is as though the good child, the house, are outside his sphere, beyond his power and ken. He is somewhere other than where he should be. Despite the thickness of his scarlet furs, the insulating girth around his middle, the heavy beard he wears, for the first time in some time Nicholas feels cold.

Those cloven hooves that pull his sleigh. They are restless. Uneasy.

Nicholas shifts the weight of his sack from one hand to the other. Its weight cuts into his shoulder, seemingly multiplying with each passing moment. This scares him the most—the sense of being slowed, weighted down. He needs to move, needs to keep moving, the icy late-December wind in his face, but his burden multiplies, and he finds himself staggering back toward the chimney from which he descended, the air around him dissipating in a vacuum of heat and shadows. And yet, when he reaches the fireplace, he cannot enter it, cannot step between its gates and fly up its flume to where his overburdened sleigh awaits. He cannot step into the fireplace, can barely travel beyond the dried-out evergreen. He tries everything: he shakes and laughs, he stares with twinkled eyes, he lays each finger aside his nose. Yet there is nothing. And when he looks down he knows why. The sound of cloven hooves fades distant.

There is ash over his suit, over his boots, but there is more on the floor. Much more. It surrounds him, a circle of dark ash from no fire he has ever seen. A perfect ring of dead ash, a barrier he cannot cross, cannot penetrate. Whoever it was that summoned him was no innocent child, no innocent baiting him his cookies. The trap was far worse than that, and its spring far more severe.

Nicholas lets out a howl, the sound of a billion children crying, the sound of merriment and mirth in its final throes. It is a cold howl, the chill of the north. And all it does is call those hooves closer.

From the shadows, they emerge. He recognizes them all, every twisted freckled face, every gap-toothed grin. They emerge with hands caked with coal dust, with the legs of insects and the blood falling from their clothes. They emerge with a glint in their eye like that of a knife, hundreds and thousands and millions of them. He recognizes every one of their faces, seen from a great distance as he moved past. And they recognize him. His face is unforgettable. It is the face in all their dreams, the culmination of every adult's glare—disapproving, distancing. They know his face all too well, have spent their lives studying it. The one last face that could show mercy but would not. Outside, the hooves clatter, anxious, too simple to know what's happened, but prescient enough to know things can never be the same.

As Eve turns to Day there is only, always, endless midnight. Tiny footsteps advance on Nicholas from all sides, chanting words in Aramaic he could not possibly know. He pleads for the sake of all the good children in the world, but the ugly grins of his summoners do not hear his bleating. Outside an icy snow falls, a heavy shroud across forever.

In the fireplace, spirits burn. The sounds of children making merry.

ALL I WANT FOR CHRISTMAS IS YOUR TWO FRONT TEETH

Jeff Strand

 ou sang the lyrics wrong," said Tiffany.

"No," said Kyle, picking up the hammer, "I didn't."

§

The first time Kyle bashed out somebody's two front teeth with a hammer, he just did it to be funny. The second time was also meant to be funny, because it was now a running gag. The same was true for the third, fourth, fifth, sixth, and seventh times. His motivation was comedy.

He didn't expect his victims to laugh, of course, though he liked to think that years later they'd run their tongue over their ceramic teeth and think, "Okay, that *was* a pretty good one."

It was a difficult gag to pull off. Even if people had been cooperative, which they weren't, it wasn't easy to specifically knock out somebody's two front teeth. Sometimes only one tooth would pop free. Sometimes he'd accidentally knock out three or four. Often they'd turn their head to avoid getting hit in the face with a hammer and he'd knock out molars instead. Once he broke some poor guy's jaw. It was a very, very imperfect process. However, he was confident that everybody understood the gist of the joke.

§

"I don't get it," said Roberta. She looked almost like her profile picture, which was a welcome change.

"The song is 'All I Want For Christmas Is My Two Front Teeth.' But I sing it as 'All I Want For Christmas Is *Your* Two Front Teeth' and then I knock out their two front teeth and keep them. How do you not get it?"

"I guess I misspoke. I get it; I just don't think it's all that funny or clever. It seems kind of mean."

"The meanness is part of what makes it so funny. It's edgy!"

"Do you only do it at Christmas?"

"Well, no, I do it year round."

"So you're saying that in July you're knocking out people's teeth with a hammer to make fun of a Christmas song?"

Kyle lowered his eyes. "There's nothing wrong with that."

"The song specifically says that all you want for *Christmas* is your two front teeth. Who the hell starts shopping for Christmas presents in the summer? That joke works from the day after Thanksgiving until December 26th and that's it."

"I get what you're saying, but it's not like I can knock out somebody's teeth and then continue the conversation as if nothing happened. Like, I wouldn't do it here. The restaurant is full of witnesses and I'm not wearing a disguise. So, no, I don't only do it at Christmas, but it's not like people forget the song exists the rest of the year. It's a classic."

"Do they lisp afterward?" asked Roberta.

"I don't know. I suppose so. Mostly they just scream."

"The whole punchline to the song is the lisp. Without the lisp the song makes no sense. Why does the kid want his two front teeth? So he can wish you 'Merry Christmas' without lisping. That is literally what the entire song is leading up to: the lisp revelation."

"I never said I was striving for one-hundred-percent

accuracy," said Kyle.

"You're bashing people in the face with a hammer for a joke, causing them extreme pain and possibly permanent disfigurement, and you can't even be bothered to be accurate to the source material? It's disrespectful. I'm not going to lie to you, Kyle—your joke sucks."

"It doesn't suck."

"It totally sucks. It's not funny enough to justify the sadism."

"I guess we'll just have to agree to disagree."

"No, you're going to stop doing it."

"Or what?" Kyle asked. "You'll call the police?"

Roberta shook her head. "I'll tell Santa Claus."

"I beg your pardon?"

"You heard me."

Kyle let out a snort of laughter. "What are you gonna do, send a letter to the North Pole? He gets a million of those a year. It'll get lost in the shuffle."

"My cousin is married to one of his elves. I can fast-track it."

"Oh." Kyle realized that he never should have confessed his secret to a woman he'd just met. He'd assumed she'd think it was funny! He never imagined she had connections to Santa Claus. Santa was a jolly old man, but he had no tolerance for physical violence, no matter how amusing.

"I have to get going," Roberta said. Since their date was scheduled to include dinner, a movie, and some light BDSM, Kyle knew she was lying.

"Don't go," he pleaded. "I made it all up. I was trying to impress you. It was a poor calculation on my part. I can't even hammer a nail without whacking my finger, much less knock out somebody's two front teeth. I'm sorry for deceiving you."

"Here's what you should do. You should kidnap them, knock them out, and let them wake up in a dentist's chair. Then you should remove their two front teeth with surgical precision. A hammer is way too sloppy. Give them Novocain so that it's scary but it doesn't hurt. After their teeth have been removed, you make *them* sing the song."

"Make them sing 'All I Want For Christmas Is Your Two

Front Teeth?'"

"No, dipshit, the real version."

"Then what do I sing?"

"You don't sing anything."

"That would mean they're delivering the joke, not me. I want to be the funny one. It was my idea. You're messing up the whole gag if it's just people missing their two front teeth singing about how they want their two front teeth. The joke is that I sing the song, and then they have this moment of realization about the horror that is about to ensue. How do you not understand this?"

Roberta shrugged. "It doesn't matter. I was kidding anyway. It's not like I was proposing a tooth-stealing crime spree with you. I'm letting Santa Claus know."

"I wouldn't, if I were you."

"Is that a threat?"

"Yes. That's why my eyes are narrowed and I said it slowly."

"You're going to kill me with a hammer in the middle of a crowded restaurant?"

"No. Of course not. That would be nuts. I'm not going to just whip out a claw hammer and start bashing your skull right here. I already said that there are too many witnesses, and I'm not wearing a disguise, and I also wouldn't have the element of surprise. That's part of why I can knock out all those teeth—people aren't expecting me to smack them with a hammer. You look like you could put up a decent fight and hold me off at least until some Good Samaritans got involved. I can fend off one or two Good Samaritans, but not three or more, and a lot of the customers in this restaurant look like the kind of people who would see a woman being attacked by a hammer-wielding madman and try to intervene. It would be absolutely insane for me to attack you right here and it quite honestly hurts my feelings that you think I'm careless enough to try such a thing."

"I was being sarcastic," said Roberta. "The tone was supposed to be 'I know damn well you're not going to try to kill me with a hammer in the middle of a crowded restaurant.' I assumed you'd pick up on that."

"Oh. Well, I didn't. You could've stopped me from doing a

long-winded explanation."

"You seemed to be enjoying hearing yourself talk."

"Please don't tell Santa Claus."

"Do you promise to stop knocking out people's teeth?"

Kyle hesitated. "Starting when?"

"Immediately."

"I ... I don't know if I can promise that. I can promise to *try*."

"Then I'm sorry. Santa Claus needs to know about this."

Kyle wanted to call her a bitch, but that would make things worse.

Of course, Santa Claus didn't bring presents to adults. His gifts only went to children whose families celebrated Christmas instead of the heathen holidays, and the quantity and quality of presents was based less on how good the children were than their socio-economic status. (Nobody was quite sure why Santa felt that rich kids should get better presents than poor kids, but that was the way it worked.)

So Kyle wasn't worried about presents. He was worried about the rumors—never confirmed—that Santa sometimes took it upon himself to punish those who were especially naughty.

The odds of Santa Claus actually coming after him were extremely remote, but it definitely made Kyle nervous. He tried to hide this by giving a casual shrug. "Well, do what you've gotta do. I can't stop you."

Roberta smiled. "Nope. You sure can't."

§

Santa Claus was one of the jolliest people in the known universe. Far jollier than God, although that wasn't saying much. He almost always had a great big smile on his face, and his belly jiggled whenever he said "Ho, ho, ho!"

Still, he had his own pet peeves. Like the way people would say, "Gosh, it must be great to only work one day of the year!" That was balderdash. He started prepping for the following Christmas on January 1st, and he didn't get any of those Monday holidays like Presidents' Day or Memorial Day off. The rumor that he just sat on a beach while the elves did all the work was simply not true. No, he didn't actually make any of the toys himself, but he functioned in a managerial capacity, making sure things got done correctly and on schedule. These were twelve-hour days, minimum. He had flaws (there was the obvious weight problem, and he sometimes fantasized about other women when making love to Mrs. Claus) but being lazy was not one of them.

That said, thanks to advances in technology, Santa had more free time on his hands. And that meant he could devote more attention to his dream of purging naughtiness from the world.

Oh, Santa took no pleasure in leaving a lump of coal in a child's stocking. He didn't giggle as he imagined that child hurrying down the staircase on Christmas morning, so excited to see what gifts he had received (and, yes, it was almost always a "he") only to discover that Santa had left no presents under the tree. He didn't enjoy the thought of the child's face falling, a single tear trickling down his face as his heart broke. It was an ugly business, but it had to be done. Santa never ate the cookies they left out—that would be too cruel.

But most of the coal children were naughty but not evil. They were the children who didn't clean their rooms, or said a bad word before they turned thirteen, or frightened their younger siblings with artificial spiders. One present-less Christmas was usually enough to change their behavior. And up until recently, that was all Santa had time to do: withhold presents.

Not anymore.

Now he occasionally found himself with enough time to pay a personal visit to a particularly naughty person. It was usually a little boy but not always. And though Santa was a jolly, friendly, lovably chubby old fellow, he could also be terrifying. Nightmarish. Demonic. And those he visited in that capacity never misbehaved again, for fear of red scaly arms breaking through the ground and dragging them screaming down into the bowels of Hell.

He wished he had more time for that.

There was a knock at the door. "Come in," he said.

Elbo, one of his worker elves, walked inside, holding a letter. "Hi, Santa."

"What can I do for you, Elbo?"

"My cousin-in-law sent me a letter. She said she went on a date with a man who is sullying the spirit of Christmas by knocking out people's teeth with a hammer."

Santa frowned. That didn't sound very Christmassy at all. "Why would he do such a terrible thing?"

"He thinks it's funny."

"Classic sadist. Well, I won't stand for that. What time zone is he in?"

"Eastern."

"So the sun sets in two hours and fourteen minutes. I'll visit him under the cover of darkness. Prepare the reindeer."

§

Kyle gasped at the sound of thumping on his roof. It couldn't be!

For a week after his date with Roberta, he'd kept a roaring fire going at all times. But he'd eventually grown complacent, and now, ten days later, he realized the error of his ways.

He heard a sound that was definitely a man sliding down his chimney.

Santa's boots struck the bottom of the chimney, stirring up a cloud of soot.

Kyle backed away in horror, hand over his mouth to stifle a scream.

Santa Claus emerged. There was a *pop* sound as his significant girth came free of the narrow chimney, but there was nothing amusing about this sound. Santa gestured, and the soot magically disappeared from beard and his red and white suit. He turned his attention to Kyle.

"Do you know why I'm here?" Santa asked.

Kyle gulped. "I'll never do it again! I promise! I've mended my ways!"

Santa cracked his knuckles. "I am capable of mercy. But did you show mercy to your victims?"

Kyle dropped to his knees. "Please, Santa! I know now just how wrong my actions were! I'll repent! I'll go to dental school, and I'll fix the teeth of the homeless for free!"

Santa raised his hands. But they were no longer hands—they

had transformed into claw hammers. The magical abilities of Santa Claus had their limits, which is why he was reliant on elves for manual labor, but changing his hands into hammers was pretty easy for him.

"No!" Kyle cried out.

Santa smashed one of his hammer-hands into a picture of Kyle that hung on the wall. "You think it's *funny* to knock out people's teeth? Do you think it'll be funny when I knock out yours? How hard do you think you'll laugh with a mouthful of broken tooth shards, huh?"

"Please, Santa! Please, please, please! Don't do it! Don't do it!"

Santa loomed over Kyle. His eyes glowed red. "Lift your face," Santa said, his voice now three octaves lower than before, and with an eerie tremor. "Lift your face and accept the punishment for your infernal naughtiness."

As tears streamed down his cheeks, Kyle looked up at him. "I'm so sorry for what I've done."

"Oh, I know you are. You're very sorry indeed. And don't think I'm going to let you keep the collection of your victim's teeth that you've acquired. That box leaves with me."

"That's fine! That's totally fine! I don't want it anymore!"

"Open your mouth. Move your lips out of the way."

Kyle, sobbing, did as he was told. "Are you going to sing the song?"

"What song?"

"The song. The song I sang. 'All I Want For Christmas Is Your Two Front Teeth.'"

"What are you talking about? I'll be honest—I didn't read the letter myself. I just let my elf Elbo summarize it. I was told that you were trying to make knocking people's teeth out with a hammer a Christmas tradition."

"I'd sing 'All I Want For Christmas Is Your Two Front Teeth' to people and then knock out their two front teeth with a hammer! It was supposed to be funny!"

"So you'd sing the classic song, but you'd swap out 'My' for 'Your,' and then you'd knock out their teeth?"

"Yes."

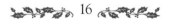

Santa considered that for a moment. "That's actually kind of clever."

"I know, right?"

"You could go to prison for it. With all of your victims, you're risking incarceration for the rest of your life. That's some *serious* commitment to a joke."

"I don't do things halfway."

Santa lowered his hammer-hands. "Look, Kyle, I'm Santa Claus. I can't give my seal of approval to the idea of you giving people bloody, toothless mouths. I need that nonsense to stop. Got it?"

"Yes, sir."

"That said, your sense of humor was in the right place. So I'm not going to punish you. Just tone it down, okay? Maybe—and I'm just spitballing here—do a variation on that thing where you say 'Got your nose!' but it's really your thumb poking through your fist. Do the song, say 'Got your teeth!' and then maybe paint your thumb white so it looks like a tooth. Both thumbs, so it's two teeth. Keep the basic joke but eliminate the grisly violence. Can you do that for me, Kyle?"

"Yes, Santa. Absolutely, Santa."

"Good. You enjoy the rest of your evening, and remember that I see you when you're sleeping and I know when you're awake, so if you use a hammer for anything but hanging a picture or building a fence, I'm coming back for you."

"Can I keep the box of teeth?"

"Yeah, sure."

Santa Claus squeezed his way back up the chimney. Kyle gazed out the window as the reindeer pulled his sleigh across the night sky, finally disappearing from sight. And Kyle, fully reformed, went to bed with a song of Christmas goodwill in his heart.

SUGAR, SPICE, AND EVERYTHING NICE

Stephanie M. Wytovich

aura Jacobson watched from the comfort of her twin-sized bed as snow collected in blankets of white on her front lawn. At eight years old, she loved Christmas and everything associated with it: hot cocoa with cinnamon, her mother's homemade gingerbread cookies—heavy with cinnamon, just the way she liked them—the twinkling multi-colored lights that dressed the house, and of course, best of all, Santa Claus.

She'd spent her evening bundled up outside, building a snowman with her older brother Theo, and now she admired the way it stood there, stoic with its ball cap, button eyes, and carrot nose as it watched her from the end of the driveway.

"You all ready for bed, kid?" her father asked as he walked into her room unannounced. He smiled and leaned down to kiss her forehead.

"Yep," Laura said, beating him to the punch as she planted a wet kiss on his lips and chuckled. "Got you! You're too slow, Dad."

She smirked, proud of her victory, but the tickle bug—her father's whimsical invention of a bug that lived in his right hand

and lived to tickle little girls—found her belly and danced as she erupted in a fit of giggles and tears as she tried to squirm away.

"All right, you win, you win!" she said, her stomach twisting in knots from laughing. "Come on, stop! I'm going to pee myself!"

Her dad laughed, forever amused at their inside joke. "Gotta watch for that bug," he said. "Little guy comes along when you least expect it."

"Yeah, yeah," Laura said, as she adjusted her shirt. "But hey, what do you think of my new jammies? Pretty *cool*, huh?"

She jumped up to model her snowflake pajama set, an early Christmas present from her mom. The two of them had been out shopping earlier that day for some last-minute presents, and when she saw the glittering shirt and pants hanging in the storefront window, she'd begged her mom to have them. "Mom says I look like the Fairy Queen. Do you know about her?" she asked, trying to sound smart.

"Know about her? Of course! She's only the prettiest, most powerful and feared woman in the Winter Realm of Mistletopia!" he said. "But let me tell you—she doesn't hold a candle to how cute you look dressed in those snowflakes."

Laura smiled, her blush reddening her already rosy cheeks. "Will you tell me about her? I want to know everything."

"Well," her father said, sitting on the edge of her bed. "The Fairy Queen is a dangerous but beautiful woman who rules over an army of Sugar Plum Fairies."

Laura's eyes grew wide. "What are Sugar Plum Fairies?"

Her father reached down and picked up Maurice, Laura's stuffed elephant, off the floor and tucked him into bed with her. "They're a breed of fae with light purple skin, big, shiny green eyes, pointed ears, and a pretty serious addiction to anything and everything sugary and sweet," he said.

"They sound nice," Laura said, her thoughts drifting to visions of a lavender creature dancing in the snow as it ate gum drops and cupcakes. "They also kind of sound like Mom."

Her father snorted and then quickly held his finger up to his lips to shush them both. He turned off the lamp on her bedside table and watched her ballerina night light come on.

"Of course they do," he said. "Because that's what they want you to think. Sugar Plum Fairies are some of the nastiest, vilest creatures around."

Now it was Laura who kept the blankets pulled up past her chin. She loved her dad's stories, even if they sometimes scared her.

"Legend has it that Sugar Plum Fairies crave the sweet dreams of children, so much so that they'll slink down from Mistletopia, climb into the ears of sleeping children, and feast on their dreams, dancing as they eat. They say if you smell sugar cookies or vanilla after the sun goes down, it means they're on their way," he said, his voice exaggerated and low for effect.

Fear settled into Laura's bones and she tightened her calf muscles.

"How do I protect myself then, Daddy?"

"Well, as long as you stay tucked into bed—" he started.

Laura's mother cleared her throat and stood in the doorway, her face a mask of anger and disappointment.

"Robert Matthew Jacobson. Are you telling her scary stories again?" she asked, already well aware of the answer. "No wonder she has nightmares."

"Oh, we're just playing around, right kid?" he said. "Nothing to be afraid of here."

He leaned down and kissed her three more times on the forehead.

She forced a smile as a pit of worry spread throughout her chest.

"Goodnight, my Lulu," he said, slipping an iron nail under her bed before walking away. He'd already fastened a horseshoe above her windowsill earlier that day when he hung the lights. "Sleep tight. Don't let the fairies bite!"

Laura watched while her mother smacked him with her oven mitt as he ran out the door laughing. She rolled her eyes, and Laura wondered if her mother sometimes thought she had two children instead of one.

"Sweet dreams, angel. Yell if you need anything," her mother said. She closed the door until only a fraction of light showed through the cracks.

Outside her window, the wind howled and shook the barren, arthritic trees on her parent's lawn. A subtle draft crept in from the cracks in the windowpane and the chill made her wish she had another blanket, not that she'd dare think about getting out of bed to get one, though.

Down the hall, Laura heard the smack of pots and pans as her mother settled back into the kitchen to bake another round of her famous Christmas treats. She had no doubt there was already a refrigerator full of fudge and butterscotch pudding, and from the fresh bite in the air, she suspected a container or two of peppermint bark was on its way.

Laura shut her eyes and prayed for nightmares.

For once, she wasn't in the mood for anything sweet.

§

Trixie and Gelsey looked in through Laura's bedroom window, their candy-cane breath fogging the glass. They'd been watching her for the past few nights, slowly taking note of what she liked, how she enjoyed spending her time, what her favorite treats were. It was important that they had as much information as possible so they could spin her the sweetest, most delectable of dreams. After all, they only had one shot, and if they screwed this up again, the Fairy Queen would freeze their wings herself.

"Look!" Trixie said, tapping on the glass. "She's holding that elephant again."

Gelsey slapped her hand. "Stop it. You're going to wake her up."

Trixie bowed her head as a wave of hurt warmed her cheeks into a dark bruise. Gelsey's tone was a bit harsher than usual, and she wasn't exactly all taffy and lollipops to begin with. Then again, she always tended to get angry when she was hungry, and the two of them hadn't had a meal since they finished off the Miller kid a few weeks back.

Her stomach growled at the memory.

The girl had tasted like orange sherbet, her dreams a merry-go-round of citrus and cream. She and Gelsey had feasted for hours, their stomachs near bursting by the time they swallowed their last bite. They'd even climbed out of her ears like two swollen bats, tired and too full to fly.

When the Fairy Queen got word of what they had done, she'd licorice-whipped them both that very night. After all, protocol clearly stated that they weren't supposed to consume flesh, only dreams; however, the two of them had clearly gotten a little carried away. By the time they were finished, the young girl's face was hardly recognizable, her eyes, nose and lips almost completely consumed.

Needless to say, the PR for the entire ordeal was a nightmare, and now more and more humans were wary of fairies, some even reverting to tricks the fae had thought were long behind them.

"Hello? Are you even listening to me?" Gelsey asked, the annoyance clear in her voice.

"Yes, of course," Trixie lied. "But maybe say it one more time just to be clear."

Gelsey rolled her giant green eyes and pointed at the window. "I'm going to cut through the glass, and then once I remove it, you need to quickly get inside and charm the parent's bedroom doorknob with a forget-me spell before we start."

"Do you think that's really necessary?" Trixie asked. It had been a while since she'd used her magic, and her heartbeat fluttered at the thought of screwing up.

"Absolutely. We can't take the chance of them seeing us feed. Didn't you hear what happened to Jitterling and Casenflugel last year?"

A look of confusion painted Trixie's face. "No? What happened?"

Gelsey slid a finger across her glittering throat.

Trixie gasped and grabbed for the window's ledge to steady herself. The world around her began to spin. Whatever acid was left in her stomach crept up her throat as steaming hot bile dribbled out the corner of her mouth. The pain was so intense, but she felt lighter, looser, the way her head felt when rushing toward a cotton-candy high. It wasn't until the beautiful freedom of free-falling through the air swept through her neon-green locks that she purpled-out and closed her eyes to the night around her.

"Trixie? TRIXIE!"

Gelsey jumped off the ledge, her wings working overtime as she desperately tried to reach her friend plummeting to the ground.

"Almost there," she said. The chill bite of air was a constant slap to her face. It nipped at her nose like a dog eager to wake up its owner. "Just a little ... bit ... farther ..."

Gelsey grabbed Trixie's arm, pulled her body close and hovered above the Jacobsons' ice-laden sidewalk, breathless and covered in sweat.

Trixie, hardly conscious, muttered something almost inaudible, her face a contorted mess of pain.

Gelsey went to set her down on a build-up of snow to assess the damage, but when Trixie's bare skin brushed up against it, steam rose from her body, her skin sizzling like butter in a hot skillet.

Trixie winced in pain. She tried to move her body but couldn't summon the strength. It was only then that Gelsey noticed the burn marks on Trixie's hand, arm, and shoulder, saw the way her skin bubbled, how boils were breaking out all up and down the side of her neck.

"Iron," Gelsey whispered, her voice peppered with concern.

Gelsey, her heart racing, reached into the black leather pouch she kept tied around her neck and pulled out a small bottle filled with lavender and aloe. She dumped a small mixture in her hand, spit in it, and then rubbed it all together into a makeshift salve. Once she was satisfied with its consistency, she gently applied it on Trixie's wounds and watched as her friend's face began to relax.

She didn't know how long she'd sat there with her; minutes, maybe hours. The night got colder, but Trixie's skin felt like fire, the fever now breaking into a sweat that soaked her hair and dripped from her eyelids.

"Come on, lady," Gelsey begged. "Stay with me."

Trixie tried to smile, but she choked, her mouth a cloud of foam, the light in her eye fading, weening, disappearing.

A tear slid down Gelsey's cheek as Trixie's muscles went slack, her arm now a dead weight held up only my Gelsey's demand.

"Don't worry, Trixie," Gelsey said, her focus now set firmly on Laura's parent's bedroom window. A pit grew in her stomach, but she smiled, her teeth dropping down into small razor-like fangs, her green eyes now black, steeped in rage. "They'll pay for what they did to you. In fact, I'll spin their dreams so sweet, they won't dare wake up until I've picked their girl's bones clean."

§

Robert and Elise Jacobson slept soundly in their beds, the glow from the television lighting their room as static climbed the walls. Gelsey watched their chests rise and fall, an accordion of breath and comfort, and then saw Elise steal the covers from her husband and wrap herself in a tight cocoon of warmth.

She chuckled to herself, forever amazed at the confidence of adults. They thought that since their childhood had long since passed that they were somehow safe and impervious to the rules and lore of fairies, of magic and monsters in the night. True, they might not taste as good with their semi-rotted meat and stress-tainted blood, but they could still feed an army should the fae be hungry enough, and while the two tossed and turned in their matching black and red flannel pajamas, Gelsey almost felt sorry for them; such easy, willing prey.

Gelsey licked her index finger and drew a small circle on the window's glass. She knocked once north, south, west, and east of the circle, and then gently blew in the center, watching as the glass shook. When a subtle pop crackled next to her ears, she pushed on the circle with all her weight and smiled as it gave in, opening like a door welcoming herself into the room.

She dusted herself off, but her ears, enchanted to detect danger, perked up as she took note of her surroundings. The house was quiet, cozy even. A trail of night lights illuminated the hallway with a dim glow, its wooden trim dusted with the remnants of loose pine needles and sap dragged in no doubt by the children's filthy feet. However, the sweeter smells in the house, those wafting in from the kitchen and living room, were almost overwhelming. A faint lingering of cranberry wove itself throughout the Jacobson's bedsheets, and in the distance, Gelsey could smell salted caramel and marshmallow, perhaps even a faint essence of chocolate raspberry, too.

Pain crept through her gums as her fangs pushed through, the hunger inside her swelling. Sweat painted her brow, the glittering of her lavender skin now sharp and blinding against the moon's light creeping in from the hole in the window.

"Not yet, not now," she said, working hard to convince herself. The allure of sugar was so intensely promising; it taunted her, assaulted her, made her question abandoning everything she was about to do. Saliva pooled in her mouth as she imagined a gluttonous binge of fruitcake and maple syrup. She wanted to rub herself sticky with whipped cream, suck on candy cane and peanut brittle until her whole body trembled, begged for release.

Like an addict, she forced herself to sit down, count to ten, to think about anything other than the sumptuous desserts set aside for family and friends, all those cookies she knew would be waiting near the tree to applaud the fat man's descent.

Breathe. Easy now. In and out.

Gelsey's jaw tightened as her fangs retracted and her body temperature cooled. She shook out her hands and tried to steady her vision, the world around her still a seesaw of blur and focus.

All right. We can do this. We've been here before, and we're stronger than whatever sugar coma is definitely waiting for us in the kitchen.

Determined, she pushed herself up off the floor, her legs wobbling like a newborn reindeer. The draft from the window curled down and threatened to wrap her in a Christmas coffin as the twinkling lights from outside the window cast Gelsey in an everchanging aura of red, green, and white.

As she readied herself for flight, the gentle hum of her wings vibrating in her ears, Robert coughed, and his body jolted into the air like an electrocuted corpse. Already on edge, this sent Gelsey into a frightfully sobering state, her tiny body now spread flat on the ground like unopened tissue paper.

Her entire body shook as she waited to see whether or not he'd hacked himself awake.

One minute passed.

Then two.

Then three, four, and five.

It has to be safe. He would have gotten up already, used the bathroom or something.

She crawled up their gray winter-themed quilt—it was still stiff and obviously newly bought—and peeked over the side of the bed.

Both of them were sound asleep, Elise's body tucked firmly against Robert's as he cradled her while she dreamed.

"Perfect," Gelsey said. She tiptoed over to them, daring herself to inch closer and closer. The dreams were always more likely to stick if she was near the bodies themselves, that way she could blow the sweetness into their ears, her hot breath a comfort as they slipped deeper and faster into her magic.

Gelsey rubbed her hands together, the heat sending purple and green sparks around the sleeping couple, her feet moving in rhythm as she began her song and dance.

"This Christmas Eve, I spin your dreams, an illusion of candy and sugar-laced creams. Drink from my fountain, get drunk on my spell, I'll sing you my secrets if you promise not to tell, for your children aren't safe, and your babies aren't sound, but look for them not, for they will never be found. Just eat from my table, listen for my bell, as you feast through the night, your children dine in Hell."

This part always made Gelsey laugh, her smirk now spreading wide across her face as she watched the sparks find their way into Robert and Elise's open mouths and ears. Her magic burrowed beneath their weighted eyelids, slid up their noses and underneath their nails, but she continued to shuffle her feet, her dance still circling the couple as their bodies relaxed and sank happily into the bed.

Only a few more minutes now ...

The Jacobsons' breathing slowed and steadied, and after a few minutes, they let out a soft whistle, the very sign she'd been waiting for. The fairies had installed this safeguard a few years ago in their magic after the aforementioned incident with Jitterling and Casenflugel, just to make sure there weren't any more causalities while hunting. Although now that she had the green light to feed, the image of Trixie's burnt body pushed itself to the forefront of her mind, her scarred and bleeding hands threatening to wrap themselves around her throat.

"Okay, okay, you're right, Trixie. It's been a while since I've properly eaten—let alone eaten anything healthy—and considering tonight's setbacks, I think a proper meal is in order to get me back on track."

Gelsey flew over and hovered about Elise's head. She plucked a hair from the back of her scalp.

"This will do just fine," she said, sucking it down like a spaghetti noodle. She felt it slither down her throat and coil in her stomach. The last time she'd toyed with this kind of glamour, she'd only had about five minutes before the effects started to take place.

A soft ticking counted down inside her head as chills swept her body and all the color drained from her skin.

"Time to go set the table," she said as she flew into the hallway, her body started to double in its size. "There's a little girl who should be waking up any minute now, and something tells me she's going to want a snack."

§

Gelsey stretched out her human-sized body and brushed a dark lock of hair out of her face, which felt lopsided and oddly tight all at the same time. She pulled a cup of steaming hot milk out of the microwave—her pallid skin now only a few shades darker than the drink in her hand—and caught her reflection in the glass. Her bright green eyes had been replaced by a pair of small, beady hazel ones, and her nose was sharp, upturned like Trixie's used to be.

Dressed in the same black and red flannel pajamas she'd seen on Elise earlier, Gelsey had fastened a hand-embroidered apron around her waist, the stitching sloppy and uneven. Part of her wondered if this was the mother's doing, or if she was gifted this poorly trimmed monstrosity as a gift.

Hideous creatures, humans are.

She set the cup on the table and squirted some vanilla extract into the foam. Next came a scoop of lavender, two cinnamon sticks, and a generous amount of her spit covered up by whipped cream.

"The perfect night-time drink," Gelsey said, confident it would work, as she sometimes drank a similar concoction before bed herself, sans fairy spit. She planned to give it to Laura after they'd had a chance to spend some time together. Help wind her down and all.

Gelsey set the cup next to a plate of white chocolate macadamia-nut bars, all the while fighting with her hair as it bounced and swung in front of her eyes with every twist and turn she made. Already nearing her breaking point in this gargantuan form, she grabbed a rubber band and tied back her long chestnut hair so she could properly set the table without dunking her split ends in every dish.

Admittedly, it took a little time to adjust to her gangly arms and size 14 waist, but she was making do with what she had to work with, and if nothing else, this body was strong, capable. She was able to carry trays of food into the next room in one trip, something she'd never think possible in her fairy form, yet here she was balancing containers of cotton-candy fudge and thumbprint cookies, apple-cinnamon pie and loaves of winterberry bread. She was hardly even tempted to feed in this new form, her willpower much stronger now that her natural fae instincts were buried under layers of flannel and fat.

"Mom?" said a sleepy, inquisitive voice. "Is that you?"

Laura walked into the kitchen, dragging Maurice by his trunk behind her.

"What are you doing?" she asked. "Wait. Did Santa come? Did I miss him"

The little girl ran into the living room and took stock of the untouched milk and cookies she'd left out a few hours before. The tree, too, remained stoic near the fireplace, its trunk a host to a selection of absentee gifts.

Gelsey watched as Laura's excitement fell, the scent of her despair a heavy musk in the air.

"Not yet, sweetie," Gelsey said, her voice deeper, huskier than her usual lilt. "But since you're up now, how about having a little snack or two with me?"

Gelsey gestured to the sumptuous spread on the table. She'd managed to add several bowls of chocolate sprinkles that sat next to fudge-dipped pretzels and strawberry ice cream. There were handfuls of gumdrops and taffy, jellybeans and toffee, and there were cookies on top of nut rolls, on top of popcorn balls slathered in chocolate and caramel.

Even the gingerbread men were twice the size of Laura's hands.

Laura's eyes widened at the multi-colored display of sugar that sat before her, the excitement so real that she couldn't possibly know where to begin.

"Are you sure?" she asked, knowing that her mother had strict rules about eating sweets after dinner.

"I think it's okay, just this once," Gelsey said. She reached out and patted Laura on the head. "After all, it's almost Christmas. It will just be our little secret."

Laura smiled and nodded her head in agreement as she reached for a handful of honey biscuits and shoved them in her mouth.

Gelsey pushed a container of hot fudge toward her. "They taste better if you dip them in this. Go ahead. Give it a try!"

Laura dunked the biscuits in the fudge and nearly swallowed them whole. Chocolate and honey smeared her lips, and Gelsey felt a familiar tingle spread through her lower half as Laura shoveled fistfuls of snowcaps in her mouth, laughing as she took advantage of her mom's sudden change of heart.

That's right, little pig. Eat up, nice and slow....

Gelsey watched as the little girl ate red bows made of Twizzlers, sucked on pop rocks and lollipops, dipped her fingers in jars of peanut butter and then covered them in butterscotch chips.

Laura licked her fingers clean, and it took everything Gelsey had not to step in and do it herself, to chomp down on those delicious slathered sausages and bite them off one by one. In fact, it was getting harder to ignore the dot of strawberry frosting she'd left on her nose, to turn away from the powdered sugar dusting her chin.

Gelsey reached for the cup of milk she'd set on the table and noticed her skin turning a soft shade of purple. Her back itched as bits of her wings started to break through the skin.

"Here, sweetheart," she said, shaking as she pushed the drink toward the girl. She felt giddy, almost nervous, as if this was to be her first time. "Wash it all down with this."

"What's in it?" Laura asked.

Gelsey felt the familiar pinch of her fangs poking through her gums. Her mouth watered as she looked at the girl: those rosy cheeks, that little potbelly. Saliva slid down her bottom lip as she imagined sucking on the girl's honey-soaked tongue.

"Mommy?" the girl asked. "Mom?"

Gelsey snapped out of it, the thought of Laura's marrow running down her throat an invitation she very much wanted to accept.

"Just—just something I like to drink when I'm winding down after a meal," Gelsey said. Her voice sounded higher now, more energetic, alive.

Laura took a sip of the drink, and then another, and another.

Gelsey watched as the girl's eyes grew heavier, grinned when she laid her head on the table, her hair soaking in a plate of blackberry jam.

"I don't feel so good, mommy," Laura said. "I think I might have a stomachache."

Gelsey cracked her neck, felt her ears sharpen to a point.

The whipping will be worth it this time.

Sharp claws poked through Gelsey's skin as she raked the glamour off her arms and legs, her body shrinking, her mouth growing wider as rows of teeth multiplied in her mouth. Memories of eating the Miller girl danced in her head—an amuse-bouche before the main course—and Gelsey found herself panting, aching, the scent of all things saccharine clinging to the girl as she moved toward her, on her, her jaw unhinged, all the light missing from her eyes as she fed.

CHRISTMAS IN JULY

John Palisano

 uzz Buy overflowed with shoppers glued to their phones, guided by the sales app like rats in a maze. Aisles displayed banners reading "Christmas in July." Put-upon spouses dragged bored kids into the maze. Chuck stood in line, third from the register, cradling his prize: a heavily discounted Instant Pot. *How the hell did I get roped into this crap?* Chuck shook his head and tapped the phone in his pocket. *Do I have enough time in this line to check my stuff before I'm at the register?* He looked up toward the register, but his eyes lingered on the woman's cleavage in front of him. She was bent over slightly, looking for something inside her bag.

Damn it. Don't do that. What are you thinking in this Me Too movement? Don't be so obvious, you creepy old bastard. Save the leering for when you're home alone looking at dirty movies on your phone. Don't do that shit public anymore. Stupid idiot. Didn't you just have a little couple time with Jilli?

He averted his eyes by trying to play it off like he was looking at his own shoes. *If anyone saw, they probably won't believe me, but maybe they'll give me points for trying.*

The cashier looked like she was going slow on purpose. She held up a crimson sweater, looked right at the price tag, turned it around and pretended she didn't know where it was.

Always getting myself involved in some girl I shouldn't be. That's my problem. Always thinking with my schmeckle. Never with my brain. Doesn't take much.

He squeezed the sides of the Instant Pot box. It's what Jillie had asked him to get for her. "Come on, sweetie," she'd said, dotting some blow into her cold-brew coffee. "Buzz Buy only has deals like this during their Christmas in July sale. And I have to work. And you're not working. And you can pick us up something for dinner."

He'd been completely naked when she brought it up. She'd just milked all the fight out of him. *She's good. I'll be stuck with her again tonight. And I'm going to be her errand boy. But I can't say no, can I? Not after the unholy act we just shared.*

"Sure, sweetie," he said.

She downed a little sip of her cold-brewed cocaine and coffee. "That's great of you," she said. "You have nothing on your schedule to do today?"

"Maybe a meeting downtown with one of the studios," I said. "Dinner with Spielberg, if I can fit him in."

She laughed. He did, too. "Seriously? You don't mind?"

"Not at all."

He flashed back to the line at the Buzz Buy. "Sir?" the cashier asked. "Are you ready?"

"Sure," he said. He placed the Instant Pot on the counter between them. He went for his wallet where Jillie's extra credit card waited.

Then the lights went out.

"Fucking LADWP," someone said behind him. "It's like *Chinatown* all over again with those assholes."

Another person chimed in. "Didn't they just give themselves a raise?"

"Ho! Ho! Ho!"

Oh, hell. This guy's going to stay in character during this. Chuck turned to the sound of the voice.

Santa's stand-in was nowhere to be seen. Instead? There was one ugly, fugly fellow standing on top of the iFlask display. He wore green with red highlights. The edges of his jacket fanned and small bells adorned each peak. His hat matched.

"You know anything about the lights?" Chuck asked. "I'd like to get home. My kids are starving." He felt his face flush. *Temper, Chuck. This is what Doctor Ding-Dong warned you about. Take it easy.*

Ugly Fugly pointed at Chuck and shook a pointed finger toward him. "I know not of the light."

Chuck pointed back. "Listen to me, you pretentious Ren Faire reject: I got places to go and people I don't want to see me in this box, so stop pointing and start fixing this so we can get out of here."

"Hey man," someone said behind him. "I don't think it's his fault."

Chuck turned and met eyes with the fellow. "I'm making it his fault," Chuck said. "What's he going to do: give us a little song a dance? That's one of the ugliest elves I've ever seen. And I've seen some ugly ass elves."

"We shouldn't be body-shaming people," the man said, shaking his box of beard oil at Chuck.

"What is this?" Chuck snatched the beard oil from the fellow. "You lubricate your beard? Why don't you rub some of this on your ass so my foot can go up it even farther, you smug bastard?"

Oil Beard stepped back and put up his hands. "I cannot believe you're speaking to me in this way."

"Oh, why don't you go and cry into your orange jeans, you beard-o," Chuck said.

"I see we have some very naughty people here with us today," Ugly Fugly said. He pointed right toward Chuck. "We don't want to be on the naughty list, do we?"

"I like the naughty list," Chuck said. "Check my browsing history. It'll make your toenails curl." He looked down. "Never mind. I'm sure your tootsies look like bacon shavings gone bad."

"Enough, big mouth," Ugly Fugly said; his voice took on an ungodly tone. The frequency cut through Chuck and made every hair on his body seem to rise. But none on his head. Those stayed put.

Ugly Fugly carried a cane. Carved from what appeared to be

bone, Chuck thought he spotted several figures sculpted around the circumference. Each seemed to be writhing in pain and in various states of torture.

"Now that's not very Christmas-y," Chuck said. "So much for peace and harmony."

Ugly Fugly lifted his cane and brought it down. The air broke with a sound like someone dropped a dozen refrigerators on the floor.

Something whizzed past Chuck.

Felt like a blast of tornado-fast air.

Someone screamed in back of him. He turned in time to see Beard Oil Man flying backward, his facial hair blown to one side of his neck. Crashing into a display of iced tea bottles, Beard Oil Man let out a high-pitched howl.

"Damn. That had to have hurt," Chuck said. "Wait. That was probably aimed at me, wasn't it?" He turned and Ugly Fugly nodded. "Where'd you learn to shoot that thing? The Stormtrooper Academy?"

The reference was lost, but Ugly Fugly raised his cane. Chuck knew he was about to shoot again.

Chuck ducked and rushed behind a display wall of speakers.

The air blast hit the display. Stuff went everywhere.

Hurrying toward the end of the aisle, Chuck raced right toward another creature that looked like Ugly Fugly. Only it was uglier. And fuglier. And bigger.

"Didn't know this was a two-for-one sale," Chuck said. "Must be my lucky day."

"You haven't been nice," said the thing.

"Who are you?" Chuck asked. "My mother?" He grabbed a speaker box off the ground and threw it at the thing. Before it had a chance to react, the box hit the creature squarely in the face. It stumbled backward.

Chuck rushed, thinking to hurry past the thing.

Something caught his eye.

A cane on the ground.

He couldn't resist.

"Come to butthead," he said, reaching down and grabbing the

cane. The thing rushed him, but Chuck moved too swiftly for it. Black blood ran down its nose. It held a claw-hand out, its fingers more pointed and longer than necessary.

Its reach failed. Chuck made it out of the way, pivoting. He felt something snap in the pit of his leg. Searing pain shot up a nerve from his pelvis, through his gut, and up into the bend of his neck. "Aw, you shit head," he said. "You made me pull my hernia." He saw red and saw it long enough to see the small cap on top of the thing's head. At first, he thought the style was something Robin Hood would wear, but then he realized what he was looking at. "What in hell? Are you some kind of an elf from hell? Or are you just a terrorist wearing makeup? That it?"

The thing lunged for Chuck. As it did, Chuck reached out for its face. "I just know you're a fake." He put his fingers into its face, making to grab some latex or rubber, but as soon as his finger hit its cheek and nose, he knew the thing was real.

That being said? The Elf-thing howled.

Chuck's fingers had hurt it.

"Gotcha right in the tenders, didn't I?"

Pissed, the Elf-thing swung fast for Chuck. He stepped backward, barely escaping the hit. He wasn't so lucky when the Elf-thing swung with its other fist.

If he'd ever been hit in the face with a catcher's mitt, he'd have felt something similar. For a moment, he saw black. Then red. Then white. Then things went back in focus. Chuck sensed pressure around his middle. He realized the Elf-thing had taken the opportunity to wrap its arms around him. It'd tried to tackle him, but it didn't quite work.

"Why didn't you go for your cane, dummy?"

He wiggled and tried to break free. Wasn't happening.

"Who you calling names?" a deep, loud voice asked.

Chuck turned. It could mean only one thing.

"Santa?" Chuck said, ignoring the struggling Elf-thing wrapped around his midsection.

Santa stood on top of a mini-stage; it looked like something the store had put together for the event, complete with cardboard winter houses and candy canes. On a sign, *December* was crossed out with a big red 'x' and *July* was written over it.

"Ho Ho," Santa said. His voice was wretched. Absolutely. "You're all getting lumps of coal today."

Of course, Santa's attention remained on Chuck and the Elf-thing. Two more elves from hell sided up alongside Santa.

"Lumps of coal?" Chuck said. "I thought you had Krampus to do your dirty work?"

"Kramp—?" Santa appeared confused.

"You know," Chuck said. "Big guy. Looks like the Grim Reaper. Eats parents. And kids." At that moment, Chuck spotted something really off about Santa. His eyes didn't shine bright like normal eyes. They looked dead inside.

Santa's skin didn't look like a person's skin; he appeared made from a jellyfish or some kind of squid. Something that was trying to look like a person.

"Hell," Chuck said. "If you're Santa Claus, then I'm Elvis Aaron Presley."

Santa was none too pleased. He raised his arms, and those arms stretched a lot longer than they should have had he been the real Jolly Old Fool from the North Pole.

At the end of his arms, his hands each split into two. Green tendrils split away from one another, twisting around, wild and free.

The Elf-thing squeezed Chuck's middle, making him cry out. He took the cane and plowed the Elf-thing's head.

It let go just enough to allow Chuck to free himself.

He stepped back. Twice.

The Elf-thing stumbled but charged again.

"Oh, no you don't," Chuck said. He pulled the display case down in between them. Stuff went everywhere. The Elf-thing was stopped long enough that Chuck made it out from the aisle, cane in hand.

He heard a loud groaning sound behind him, coming from the stage. Before he could turn to look, one of the Elf-things got in front of him.

Chuck looked around. "Where the hell did everyone go?" He couldn't see any of the other customers. *Where's the girl I was checking out? Where's Beard Oil Boy?* He spotted the cashier, ducking behind the counter, watching them with her nervous eyes. "You!" Chuck said. "A little help in aisle 14, please?"

The cashier didn't budge.

The Elf-thing did, lunging for Chuck.

Chuck swung out of the way but still smelled the creature. "Jesus. You smell like a can of dogshit and horseshit. How'd you manage that combo?"

A second swing also missed Chuck.

He whacked the cane on top of the Elf-thing's head. It howled and put its claws to the hit. "Knick-knack, paddywhack, jackass."

Chuck rushed away from the creature.

He gave the middle finger to the cashier. "Your customer service sucks." He saw the Instant Pot still on the counter. *Mental note. Don't forget that. Jillie will be waiting.*

Something stuck into the back of Chuck's neck. Like a bee sting. Coated with salt.

"F-uck," Chuck hollered, reaching behind with his left hand on instinct, still holding the cane with his right.

Whatever had stung him was still connected. Like a wire. Like a ...

It jerked him, lifting him off his feet and several feet, landing Chuck on his back.

His neck killed from the pull. Everything hurt.

The tendril pulled him.

Every tug made pain fire explode from the back of Chuck's neck all throughout his body. *Whatever you do, don't let go of the cane.*

Santa Thing reeled Chuck closer.

"What the hell do you want?" Chuck hollered through the pain.

Santa Thing seemed to be through speaking English and answered him with an unnatural, guttural sound. *It sounds like a bison with an upset stomach. Maybe it's hungry and wants to eat me.*

The Elf-things closed in on Chuck, too. He saw the one he'd beaned step up, still rubbing its misshapen noggin.

He looked upside down and saw Santa had lost all pretense about being a person. The skin ... or whatever its covering had been ... had split into pieces. Underneath he spotted a pale, semi-translucent creature.

And it pulled him closer.

Santa Thing was in full bloom. His tendril arms were waving in the air, spinning. Santa Thing's maw opened, showing off lots of little triangular, razor-sharp teeth.

"You are hungry, aren't you?"

Another jerk and Chuck was almost under Santa Thing.

The teeth glistened. He swore he saw its tongue licking the insides of its mouth in anticipation of its meal.

"If you eat," Chuck said, "that means you've gotta have the plumbing." He took the cane in both hands and drove it upward as hard as he could.

Right into Santa Thing's crotch.

It connected.

Santa Thing howled like all the hounds of hell. And maybe one lone cat from hell, too.

"Gotcha," Chuck said. "Knew it."

He pulled the cane back and shoved it up a second time.

More screams.

The point sticking into the back of his neck freed up. Chuck took the chance and popped up as fast as he could, pulling the cane down and using it as a crutch. The point of entry at the back of his neck stung. His body hurt worse than ever, but he pushed right through it.

As soon as he had his bearings, Chuck swung the cane as hard as he could at Santa Thing's head.

To his surprise, the cane seemed to go right through Santa Thing's head. For a split second, Chuck even felt bad. *What have I done? I just killed Santa Claus.*

Santa Thing's head split open. *That was easy. Like batting a cake made of jello.*

The gooey insides splattered all over the place. The Elf Things cried out and up their arms.

Without much of a working head left, Santa Thing dropped. Chuck nudged it with the toe of his sneaker. It didn't move. Looked dead as dead can be.

Chuck looked around. "Everyone can come back out now," he said. "I saved the motherfucking day." He held the cane up high.

Silence.

The Elf Things backed away.

Someone crept out from behind a display of internet-connected tricycles. Then more people came out from hiding. He still didn't see Beard Oil or the woman he'd oogled.

"You ... killed ... Sanubis," someone said.

"Who?" Chuck asked.

"Sanubis," another said. "God of gifts and light."

Chuck shook his head, regarded the mess of a creature in front of him. "That thing?" he said. "It was going to eat me. Its friends attacked me. It ..."

"He was only playing," said a woman approaching him. She looked normal, other than appearing abnormally pale. "And now you killed him."

The Elf Things hung their heads. Defeated.

"Are you kidding me?" Chuck said. "How come no one stepped up and said anything? Why'd you let me?"

"It happened too fast," the pale woman said.

Chuck sighed. "No way," he said. "It stung the back of my neck. It dragged me toward its mouth. Doesn't make sense."

"He liked you," she said. "That's how we all ... became us."

Chuck stormed away. "You cult-y freaks can have him. Or what's left of him. You should have let me know before I took off his head. You have to ask before you stick your stinger in someone's neck."

He clicked the cane against the floor as he walked. Once he made it to the counter, he grabbed the Instant Pot. He turned to them. "I'm taking this in lieu of suing you all for assault and battery," he said. "We'll call it even-steven, okay?" He hurried toward the door.

"Wait ... sir ... there's something you should ..." the pale woman said.

"I don't care," Chuck said on his way out the door. "You ungrateful pack of freaks." He shot them the bird to punctuate his exit.

 41

§

Chuck unlocked the front door of the apartment slowly. He heard that old '70s disco they both loved cranking up from inside. "Oh, yeah, baby's waiting for me."

He was so excited getting through the door, he nearly dropped her Instant Pot.

Inside her heard sounds other than the music.

Cries.

Is she hurt?

He rounded the corner of the living room toward. Didn't see her. Heard her. Recognized the sounds for what they were.

Please just be watching something naughty. Damn it. Don't be with someone else.

She'd shut the bedroom door. *Not a good sign.*

The sounds of sex were louder. *Well, it sure sounds like her. Maybe she's just pleasuring herself real loud. Waiting for me. Getting ready.*

As soon as Chuck opened the door, he saw four legs going every which way. A guy's butt going back and forth on top. His sag shack swung to and fro. Jillie under him. Moaning. Loving it.

Fuck.

Chuck snuck up behind them as quiet as he could. Spotted her coffee mug on the side table, the top still rimmed with just a little hairline of coke.

When he was within striking distance, he smacked the guy's ass mid-thrust as hard as he could.

It instantly killed the mood.

"What the fuck?" the guy said. He pulled out and turned around. Saw Chuck. "Who the hell?" He looked like a low-rent anime cosplayer, complete with swooshy black hair and pursed red lips. His weiner shrunk into a little baby carrot in a blink.

"Oh, Chuckie," Jillie said. "What took you so long?"

Chuck shook his head. "You asshole," he said. "After what I went through to get you that stupid Instant Pot."

She didn't even bother trying to get up or cover herself. "Come on, baby. It's not like we were exclusive or anything. We never said we were."

"You're right. I just live here. With you. That's all."

"We have an open relationship."

"And it just opened up a whole lot more," Chuck said. "I'm going to take off for a while. I'll be back for my stuff at some point."

He leaned down and smacked the guy's ass even harder.

"Dude!" the guy said. "What's your problem?"

"Give her one from me," Chuck said. "You stupid, pretty moron. Be a shame to stop now after all that work."

He went back to the living room, the sounds of Jillie calling for him in the background. He took the Instant Pot, put it on the ground, and kicked the box with all he had. "Try returning that," he said.

Chuck left.

He saw red. Then black. Then white. Then red again.

Chuck recalled the pale lady from Buzz Buy. "Wait ... sir ... there's something you should ..."

Mamma always said I was lucky. Lucky Chuck. I'm not sure about that. Sometimes? I think I'm anything but Lucky. And I swear? This stuff always seems to start with me and some girl.

Outside, he raised his head and eyes toward the blazing midday sun. As he did, he thought he saw shapes moving behind his eyelids. The organic reds and yellows one normally sees moved and turned into wiggling things ... things that started to sing.

The back of his neck where he'd been stung responded. It hurt for a moment, then it started to feel different. It started to feel good.

Over the top of the apartment building, between the rows of palm trees, backlit by the midday summer sun, Santa Thing arrived in a magic sleigh. Painted black with white trim, the sled bucked as the reindeer trotted through the sky. Their bodies had holes where they were partially decomposed.

Chuck imagined that snow blew around, but as it reached him, he realized it was not frozen water but the remnants of an epic fire. Ash blew, and the blue sky turned orange and red. Chuck coughed as the ash overtook his sinuses and throat. His eyes watered, but he still made out Santa Thing high above, staring him down. Its eyes were grey and blank. Its expression null. Somehow, its intent came through clear. It wanted Chuck.

Taking out a long scroll, Chuck knew it had to be a list of names. Santa Thing pointed at one then pointed at him.

His throat tightened more. He clutched it.

Coughed.

Couldn't stop coughing until he doubled down.

It's trying to kill me. Suffocate me.

He shut his eyes. Counted backward from ten—a trick he learned to sober up just enough when he needed it, even if it only worked for a few minutes. *Calm yourself. That's the only way this is going to work.*

Standing upright and opening his eyes, Chuck breathed in. As lightheaded as he was, he was relieved to find Santa Thing and his Pain-deers had vanished. The sky had returned: big, blue, endless and unforgiving. *Was all in my head. Maybe? Who knows. Get out of here for now.*

As he walked to his car, Chuck wondered where he was going to go and what he was going to do. "Ain't sure about nothin'," he said. "But I sure as hell know it ain't ever going to be the same. I ain't feeling so lucky now, Mamma."

He turned because he heard his name.

Jillie.

She stood alone on the balcony, calling him.

Seeing her pulled him right out of whatever it was he'd been tripping on.

He gave her the finger.

"Merry Christmas," he shouted. "And Happy fucking New Year."

The End.

For now.

THE EVER GREEN

James Chambers

hristmas came cruel that year.

Having spent weeks in town shopping, the man who called himself Master Wenzel arranged wrapped gifts beneath the balsam pine he'd ordered cut from the edge of the woods and then had me light the candles he'd pinned to its branches. Satisfied, he settled under blankets by the window overlooking the manor entrance to watch for his family. Beyond the short gravel tongue from the front door, though, a blizzard erased the world outside. "Bells of Christmas" played on the phonograph while snow fell and wind howled, and we awaited arrivals I knew could never occur. Such is the power of the mind to deceive itself that the Master, humming along to one of his favorite Christmas melodies, so persevered in his hope that I had not the heart to take it from him.

Resigned, I visited the pantry to refresh our tea and brandy.

Moments later he cried out for me, "Neale!"

His wood-crack voice jolted me so that I spilled boiling water on my hand.

"Neale, come fast!"

Biting back a groan at my endless ineptitude in the kitchen, I wrapped a tea towel around my blistering knuckles before dashing

45

to his side. He stood wiping the fog from the window with an embroidered handkerchief.

"Look! There's a man by the trees."

I squinted until, by an inexplicable trick of nature, the gray, burdened clouds parted and permitted silver streaks of moonlight to caress the earth. In their watery illumination appeared a man, bulked with a long green coat. He dug into winter's blanket for wood, which he gathered to his chest. His gangly legs carried him spider-like among the drifts, and the clumsy movements of his arms reminded me of inchworms and caterpillars.

"Who is he, Neale?"

"I don't know, sir."

The man's hood hid his features—yet a creeping sense of his awareness of us observing him set my hairs on end, as if his unseen eyes perceived us and his muffled ears heard our every word. He flickered in wind-driven snow squalls.

"Who could he be so desperate on this Christmas night that he collects wood wet from the snow?" the Master said.

"I'm unsure, but ... perhaps the man who lives in the cottage by the old church with the fountain."

"St. Agnes' Church?"

"Yes, St. Agnes' caretaker. That's who it could be."

"Poor devil, although I admire his determination. Still, it pains me to see him suffering the cold while we sit here by the fire, and Madam Wenzel and the little ones enjoy a Christmas feast at the Waldorf-Astoria while your son and his brood are ... are ... Neale, I'm sorry, but I've forgotten your family's plans this Yuletide."

"The same as yours, undoubtedly, spending Christmas sheltered from the storm."

My words rang true enough in a literal sense.

"Yes and we shall celebrate with them on the Feast of St. Stephen when all this terrible bluster and snow expires. Perhaps we should invite the man in?" He leaned to the window, smile faltering. "Ah, damnation! He's gone, swallowed up by the storm. He's going to have a devil of a time warming himself with wet wood." He resumed his chair and blankets. "Play 'Bells of Christmas,' Neale, and be swift about it. I've been waiting all night to hear it."

I restarted the record for the third time that night and then fetched the Master's tea. When the record finished playing once again, he fell deeply asleep. I extinguished the candles on the tree and then placed three logs on the fire to fight the chill that blanketed the house, so much of it closed for so long that properly heating the open rooms remained a constant challenge. Tucking two blankets around me, I reclined in a chair by the hearth. As I lingered on the cusp of sleep, melancholy transformed the wind's lilt into the voices of my daughters singing carols as they had as girls, so bright, so musical, when Christmas had ignited in them that special fire of wonder that burns only in children. So very long since I had last heard them.

Later the Master's booming voice awoke me.

"Up, up, Neale!" he said. "We have an errand of mercy to perform!"

Throwing off my blankets, I lurched to my feet. The Master stood framed by the window, spectral in the dying firelight.

I reached for a fresh log to throw on the flames.

"Forget that, Neale. Gather our coats and meet me in the pantry."

"What is it?"

"You know better than to dawdle, man. Do as I say!"

He splashed the contents of his mug onto the embers, raising a cloud of hissing steam, then stamped from the room. I soon joined him in the pantry where he worked at packing much of our Christmas provisions into two wicker picnic baskets. He wrapped an entire cooked ham in wax paper, then loaded it alongside tins of creamed herring, cranberries, olives and plum pudding, boxes of cookies and biscuits, and three bottles of spiced wine. He bade me carry it all to the garage, an awkward task with my injured hand, and load it into his favorite vehicle, the Bull Dog. There he met me with two canvas-bound bundles of wood, which I stowed with the baskets in the trunk while he threw open the carriage doors, letting in bitter cold air.

"The storm has paused. We must help that caretaker who lives in the cottage."

Although the snowfall had ceased, the prospect of driving in the gusty, snow-blanketed night worried me. "I pity the man as much as you, but—"

The Master thumped the Bull Dog's fender twice.

"She'll get us there and back again, Neale. You're not frightened, are you? Don't you trust her engine and axles?"

The munitions company from which the Wenzel fortune flowed had produced the unique vehicle in the midst of the Great War, intending to provide swift, armored, all-terrain transport for officers and couriers, but the war ended before production began, and so the prototype came home to the family estate. The clanking assemblage of treads, skids, and tires persisted as part of the manor fleet. Many years past, it had been a great thrill for the children to ride it through the woods.

The engine clanked and grumbled as the Bull Dog rolled from the garage. Wind shook the carriage. Ice crystals rattled on the windows. Snow tugged at the wheels, but the treads bit back and kept us rumbling along course as the manor house fell from sight and the woods deepened. The Master slowed as we passed the solemn plot of land east of the main drive. His gaze, like mine, turned to the weary stone markers jutting from snow mounds within the confines of a wrought-iron fence. For a moment, I hoped the sight might restore his sense of order and reality so that we could turn back, but with a determined grunt he only pressed onward faster.

Clouds strangled the moon. A few snowflakes spiraling past the headlights' glare became granular white cataracts baffling our view. The storm rocked the Bull Dog and raged again in all its fury, which soon overwhelmed even the Bull Dog's prowess. It shuddered through deepening drifts, its engine growling until the front bumper thumped against a snow-draped obstacle, and we ground to a stop. Attempting to reverse from the obstruction, we only skidded sideways and sank deeper in the snow, firmly stuck.

"The cottage can't be far," he said. "Come, Neale, let's not surrender to this storm."

With that he exited the car and rummaged the baskets from the trunk. He opened my door and then pushed one into my arms. We each slung a bundle of firewood from our shoulders.

"We should stay with the Bull Dog!" I called over the freezing wind. "Run the engine for heat and wait for morning."

"Nonsense," he shouted. "Are you too timid to perform your duty to your fellow man in a little snow? For God's sake, Neale, it's Christmas. Stop thinking of yourself."

At that we trudged into a world churning white. Snow crusted my eyelids. My pace slowed with each step as the cold numbed my feet, and I fell behind.

"Don't flag now, Neale," the Master said. "Follow my footprints. Go where I lead!"

Stretching my gait to match his robust stride, I stepped in the hollows he left in the snow and maintained my pace. Still, I couldn't keep up with him, and he soon hiked beyond my sight. The basket weighed heavy in my grip, my wounded hand throbbing with needles of pain.

We had driven much farther than I thought, because after several more minutes of trailing the Master, lights appeared, framed in the windows of the cottage by Saint Agnes' Church. Tracks led me to the open front door, where warmth and illumination bled out. Holly wreaths, tied to either side of the entrance, gleamed green and red, and a matching garland hung above it.

I entered—and dropped the basket and firewood in shock.

A fire roared beyond a stone hearth and gave off a cloying, stifling heat. The Master, seated on a rough-hewn stool, stared into the flames as if mesmerized—and wept. Tears streaked his cheeks. His basket lay spilled at his feet, the ham and wine bottles scattered. A Christmas tree in the corner presented a most horrendous sight. Garlands of teeth, animal skull ornaments, ribbons of knotted hair, and atop it a silver star as large as a dinner plate, polished to mirror smoothness. It cast the unnatural firelight throughout the room.

"Welcome! And good cheer to you!"

I spun around.

Behind me stood a man wearing a mask of carved bark. Hollowed-out knots formed sockets for eyes that glistened like ice-sheathed holly berries. Creases in the grain marked a lipless mouth outfitted with stubby, brown teeth. Mistletoe spread from his scalp. He wore a lush forest green coat with ermine cuffs, its deep hood folded back on his shoulders, hem brushing the floor, the very the coat we had seen from the manor window.

Eying the items at my feet, he said, "Thank you for your generosity."

The origin of his accent eluded me.

"Who are you?" I said.

"I am the Ever Green. This night once belonged to me."

"What is wrong with the Master?"

"He looked in the silver star."

I shook the Master by the shoulder, but his fixation never wavered from the flames.

"He did not like what he saw. Would you like to look?"

I glanced at the star mirror. "What did he see?"

"True things."

A cold blast roared through the door, setting off shivers within me.

"I see you know what truths he witnessed," the man said. "Why then do you serve him?"

"He's better than most, no worse than any other. Hasn't he shown you kindness tonight?"

"Yes, but what kindnesses has he shown you?"

"Too many to number over the years."

"Oh? When your eldest son died fighting in France, did he comfort you? No, he lectured you on sacrifice and duty, on honor and country, while his family's treasure fattened on the Great War, and he himself lobbied for raising aggression, for more and better weapons, more death."

"How ... could you know that?"

"When the influenza claimed his wife and daughters did he thank you for the hours you spent tending him even though he kept you from your second son's side while he too perished from the disease? Did he offer you time to grieve when your wife succumbed to tuberculosis or your third son's widow and your grandchildren died in the fire that consumed their home this past summer? Your last joys in the world taken, while all the years of your service he has treated you as a tool like his stranded car."

"Who ... are you?" I said. The man stepped closer, the aroma of pine wafting from him. He backed me against the wall and regarded me with an icy stare. "Sir," I said, "if you would speak to me I beg you remove that awful mask and show me who you are!"

"But, my kind gentleman, don't you see that I wear no mask?"

The truth of it dizzied me. He stared at me with his naked, mysterious, inhuman aspect. A face born in the old woods and the deep past, the features of a thing that would live always when other life slept through the cold and dark.

"What are you? Why are you doing this?" I said.

"These cold, lonely nights belonged to me long before you claimed them for your Savior. Your master raised a tree in my image, decorated it with glitter and bows, and lit it with candles. He called on my spirit as a reminder of life and light in the winter's dark. The green bough that bends but never perishes. I have answered his plea and choose to judge the worth of his gifts."

"His mind is not sound. Delusion rules him. How can you judge a man in such a state?"

"His sins and actions are his own. But *you* may leave. I grant you my blessing to return safely to your manor."

The open door tempted me. My heart ached for the night, for the ice and snow, none of which frightened me as much as the Ever Green.

"I won't leave without him."

"Why such loyalty?"

"It's Christmas. One must show compassion."

"Midnight has passed. Now is your feast of St. Stephen, where the master serves the servant, a celebration I once knew as the Saturnalia. It is you who receives the gifts this day. Take the one I offer you on your master's behalf."

I gripped the Master's shoulder. Wracked with sobs, he shuddered at my touch and looked away from the fire, staring at me with teary eyes.

"My heart is breaking," he said. "I don't understand how these awful visions can be true. Are they truly taken from us? Do they truly lie beneath that patch of ground we passed? I am lost, broken. How can I go on? Oh, leave me be. Accept the gift. Go before you can never leave."

The Ever Green grabbed my wrist, his grip coarse and sticky with pine sap. He removed my glove then unwound my tea towel bandage. His twiggy fingers smeared sap on my reddened skin and blisters. Seared hairs regrew and scalded flesh vanished, replaced by new.

"Receive our gifts. You may leave freely."

"What happens to the Master if I do?"

"I shall judge him. His spirit will feed the Ever Green."

"God help me, I can't take his gift or yours. You've made a mistake. He's given me all the gifts I can bear, over and over his entire life, more than I or anyone ever deserved—and this last gift I cannot accept!" My heart jumping, I faced the Ever Green, a thing part of my brain screamed could not exist though it stood right before me. "For he is not the true master here!"

"Does he not order and control you?"

"Yes, but that is how I wish it. When the last of his family died in the summer fire, his mind cracked. He no longer knows who he is. He is Neale and I Wenzel, but in the delirium of his grief he came to believe ... that he is *me!*"

"You are the true Master Wenzel?"

"I was. I am. My family is long dead, and when Neale's mind broke at the loss of what remained of his, I saw myself through his eyes for the first time. All those things of which you accuse him are true—but I did them to him! I serve him because he could not accept the tragedy of his life and retreated into mine to justify all he had sacrificed for me. His entire life dedicated unjustly to mine. I humble myself in gratitude for his service, which I never appreciated when it was given. Please don't ask me to accept any more from him than I already have. I owe him so much I can't bear to increase the debt."

"This then is your gift to him, the blessing of the master to the servant?"

"Until he regains his mind or one of us dies, yes."

The Ever Green released me.

"It is well you spoke true to me for this I knew the moment you crossed my threshold. Your gift is honorable and worthy. Go now and be merry, if you can."

The Ever Green waved his gnarled fingers past my face.

The next moment darkness and heat blanketed me, obliterating all my senses. When they cleared, the sun pressed at my eyes. I awoke stiff and cold in the Bull Dog's passenger seat. The storm clouds had fled the sky, and dawn light dazzled the snowy woods. Voices spoke outside the car, where Master Wenzel stood with the old man I knew as the true caretaker of St. Agnes.

"Come, Neale, we survived the night thanks to your advice to stay with the Bull Dog. The caretaker found us while scrounging for wood. His cottage is only yards away, but we'd never have found it in the dark. He's invited us in. Put yourself to use and let's reward him with a feast and a fire!"

While Master Wenzel walked on with the old caretaker I noticed as I gathered the baskets and wood from the Bull Dog's trunk that my burned hand remained healed. The heavy packages weighed me down in the shadows of the snow-tipped pines, but so long as I stepped where Master Wenzel had stepped I found the burden much lighter.

WELCOME TO THE PARTY, PAL

William Meikle

e finally got the kids to bed near midnight but not before we'd watched and sung along to Albert Finney, then Michael Caine as Scrooge, the latter twice. By then Jo was dead on her feet, but her twin brother Duncan had fire in his eyes; he'd been told earlier in the week at school that Santa Claus wasn't real, and he was determined to know, one way or the other. As I sat on the sofa with Elaine for our own annual ritual movie, I imagined Duncan's blue eyes staring hard at the ceiling in the room upstairs. He would be straining for any indication of sleigh bells in the wind or reindeer on the roof; he was still young enough to want to believe.

We had a jug of mulled wine, a bottle of expensive vodka, and a round of nice aged brie. I had stoked a roaring fire into life with judicious use of the old iron poker, and we had hours to ourselves, at least until Duncan's itch got too much for him and he and his sister, descended on the presents under the tree like hungry raptors. I intended to make the most of it.

Elaine, as ever, had fallen under the movie's spell from the first few scenes, and I caught myself joining her in mouthing the dialog as the bad guys crashed the party.

"Mr. Takagi, who said we were terrorists?"

As I reached for my glass to toast the clock above the mantel ticking over into Christmas Day, I heard a dull thud from somewhere overhead.

"The old man's early," I said, but Elaine's smile quickly turned to a frown as the noise was repeated, heavier this time, and the frame of the house shook, setting the light fitting overhead swinging.

"There's somebody up there," she said, barely more than a whisper. The barefoot man on the screen seemed to answer.

"No fucking shit, lady. Does it sound like I'm ordering a pizza?"

But by that time I was on my feet and heading for the stairs, a vague, almost floating, feeling of dread washed through me as there was another, even louder thud and the house shook again. I intended to head for the kids, but I never made it across the room.

Ash and soot fell in a rush down the chimney, sending a billowing cloud of black smoke and choking fumes across the room. I heard a rasping, cloth on stone, then felt hot sparks lash my cheeks. There was a thud, a flare of red as something heavy landed in our fire from above. I had to rub my eyes against a sudden, almost acidic, sting, and when I opened them it was to see a tall bulky figure standing among what were now embers on our hearth.

Elaine screamed and I heard a squeal from Duncan upstairs. In his case it sounded more like delight, but whoever—whatever—this was, it was no Santa Claus. It carried an empty burlap sack over its left shoulder and wore a heavy coat of reddish-brown matted fur—at first I thought was part of it but the coat swung open at the front revealing a gray, painfully thin body. The ribcage, pelvis and legs looked almost canine-—wolf-like even, but the head end was more goat-like, with tall, curving horns that scraped our ceiling. No goat ever had teeth like this, though—pointed, fang-like, with a silvery hue that seemed almost metallic.

The blessed Bruce spoke on the screen.

"Come out to the coast; we'll get together, have a few laughs."

The thing on our hearth raised its snout and brayed out a laugh in reply, although I heard little humour in it.

"Santa Claus!" a small voice shouted on the stairs. My head turned the same time as the thing's and we both stared at Duncan who had already come down four steps before stopping, a confused look in his eyes.

"Beep! Would you like to go for double jeopardy where the scores can really change?"

The thing in the hearth smiled—don't ask me how I knew, it was something in its eyes, something in the way it rolled a fleshy tongue over its teeth. It stepped away from the fireplace and began to head toward the stairs where Duncan stood, frozen in place.

"No!" Elaine shouted. "Leave my boy alone."

I finally found that I could move. I waited until the beast walked passed me then stepped over to the fireplace and took up the iron poker. I turned to my wife.

"Hey babe, I negotiate million-dollar deals for breakfast. I think I can handle this Eurotrash."

I went after it and caught it on the stairs, three steps below Duncan, just as it was opening the black mouth of the burlap sack. The poker whistled in the air as I smacked the beast on the back of the head with all my strength. It was like swinging a hammer against solid rock, a jarring thrum running up my arm and across my chest. But it had served a purpose. The beast stopped heading for Duncan and slowly turned toward me.

"Welcome to the party, pal."

I thrust the poker like a sword, under its ribs. The blow didn't penetrate the skin, but the beast staggered. It didn't fall, so I hit it again, a backhand from below my waist level, heading up and hitting the sweet spot on the point of its chin. Its head jerked back, it staggered again and almost fell. I kicked it where its balls should be, then yelled, screaming nonsense words as I rained blow after blow on its head and shoulders.

It crept away from me, heading for the fireplace and escape.

Elaine stepped forward and mashed a slab of runny Brie in its face. It mewled, clawing at suddenly blinded eyes and I stepped up my attack, driving it backward. I paused only to pick up the bottle of vodka with my free hand as I backed the beast against the embers of the fire.

I shouted, more incoherent nonsense, and dashed the vodka at its feet.

It went up in flames in seconds. Even then it tried to reach the chimney to flee, but the iron poker kept it down, pinning it in the flames until its struggles lessened, grew feeble and finally, with a crumble of ash falling in on itself, ceased entirely.

"Yippee-ki-yay, motherfucker," the Blessed Bruce said.

I agreed with him.

CHRISTMASSACRE™: THE LAST CHRISTMAS

Jason V Brock

I

Christmas Eve—11:58 PM: **Rise of the Elves**

"Drop it, fat man!"

The elf's plump fingers tightened the tinsel rope around Mrs. Claus's neck: "I *mean* it."

Santa Claus lowered his gingerbread axe, face a mask of rage. Coagulating blood from his nose had tinged his beard crimson; bits of shattered candy and bright-orange elf gore adorned his vibrant red suit and dripped from the weapon by his side. His hair was a wild corona of tangled locks, gray and wispy around his sweat-slicked pate.

"After all I've done.... How *dare* you turn on me."

The elf, Alexander, laughed, a croaking wet sound. "Life's a bitch, what can I say, Claus?" Mrs. Claus's reddened eyes bulged slightly as she struggled against the garrote of silver holographic decoration he pulled around her delicately veined throat.

Blocking the doorway, two other rough-looking elves he did not recognize, in threadbare striped socks and filthy overall shorts, stared at the old man, their breath billowing heavily in the frosty air. Around them, the house was in shambles—candy-glass windows broken, the door blown from its ice hinges by a chocolate bomb. Frigid pumpkin-scented air was filling the place, which looked more like some destroyed safehouse in a war zone than a snug cottage from Currier and Ives. Sad fragments of broken toys and the wish-filled letters of desperate children littered the floor, trampled under the elves' curly-toed booties like so much repressed trauma and neglect.

"What ... what do you want, Alex? More time off? Medical leave? What?"

The elf narrowed his slanted eyes. "You killed my buddies, Claus," he said, nodding his head toward the disjointed bodies on the floor of the living room.

"Yes. I did. When the chocolate bomb blew the door off, I ... I panicked. I still don't understand why you're attacking me—"

"Come off it!" Alexander raged, his pupil-less black eyes widening in his pallid face. "You know *why*, you fat bastard! We've gone over this for decades, and you keep ducking the issues. We break our *tails* while you eat bonbons and vacation in Switzerland most of the year with," he glanced down at his prone captive, jerking the tinsel taut for emphasis, *"this* one." He looked at the old man again. "Does she *know*, Claus? About the other women? The dope?" His lips peeled back, revealing rotted dentition from eating too many sweets.

Santa was now sweating in the arctic air, nervously casting his gaze between the elves and his wife's haunted expression. *"That's not true!* He's making that up!"

Alexander's smile faded. "Oh, it's true, *fatso*. And it's true that you keep us hooked on the candy, too. You *knew* we were sugar addicts, Claus. How could you prey on our genetic weakness like that? Just to keep us working in your slave factory. How debased *are* you, fat-ass?"

Tears welled in Santa's eyes. He had noticed the discontent building, but never expected it to boil over like this. And so close to Christmas, the most wonderful time of the year for their enterprise. He was sure that Krampus, Black Peter, and the rest of the Yule

Board would act on this once he returned from his flight. Next week there would be hell to pay for letting this little insurrection come to pass ... but for the time being he was going to have to accept the reality of the situation and get airborne as quickly as possible. Every lost moment had to be made up with flight speed and efficiency inside the homes as he delivered presents. No time for any kinky dalliances with hard-up negligee-and-garter-clad big-titted MILFs this year, and no time for any foolish loitering with the "funny" brownies and cookies, either. *Strictly business.*

"Alex—I understand. But we need to get this show on the road ... once I return, we can—"

The elf snorted. "We can discuss things, right? Like all the other times? Yeah ..." his voice trailed off. "Let's see, shall we? Let's see how it all goes. But, I'm warning you, Claus...." Alexander leaned in, pulling the tinsel tight. Mrs. Claus seemed to be getting drowsy. "When you come back, things are going to change."

Santa swallowed. Alexander relinquished his hold on Mrs. Claus, and she collapsed onto the floor completely, gasping for air and coughing. The three elves stepped aside so that Santa could exit his home. Outside the door he could see his sled—loaded with bulging sacks of gifts—waiting for him. The reindeer team was covered in blood, skin hanging from their bodies, bones exposed, yet still mobile. He shot a stunned look at Alexander.

"They're dead, yeah. But we brought 'em back so you could make your rounds. You know—*elven magic*, Claus. Not that stupid Keebler crap. *The real deal.*"

Santa nodded slowly. From his pocket, he retrieved his hat and pulled it onto his head. He looked at his wife, bending down to touch her tear-tracked cheek with his bloody hand. She took it in hers and kissed it, locking her gaze with his and trying to smile through her shock and anguish. Standing, he walked to the bobsled, climbed in.

In the dark, wintry night, the sleigh bells rang out in a minor tone as Santa took to the skies, the cold rays of a full moon silvering his luge. He wept in the silent night, finally choking out a somber "Ho, Ho, Ho ..." before accelerating to the speed of light and puncturing the spacetime continuum.

It was going to be an exceptionally long holiday.

II

Christmas—Daybreak: **Special Deliveries**

While tiny tots everywhere rushed to claim gifts under Christmas trees that morning, it gradually dawned on people that this was a very different kind of Yuletide celebration. While the children tore into the gaily wrapped offerings, and parents—new cell phones in hand—joyfully recorded many a first Christmas, little did anyone know they were also witnessing the very last one.

In home after home—whether the U.S. or Europe, from South America to Australia, the Middle East and Africa, Asia and beyond—throngs of innocents would discover horrors beyond belief in the bloody hours to follow. What only scant moments prior had been described as "breathtaking"—simple displays of tranquility and serene family communion—gradually degenerated into anguished scenes of outright carnage and unmitigated brutality as humanity collectively began to understand the ironic literalness of that descriptor.

The day dragged on, with scattered reports of isolated "gift mishaps" giving way to steady grim accounts of mass death in urban centers and rural settings alike. Broadcast coverage of mutilation and examples of "toy terrorism" surged in from social and traditional media across the globe; in the torturous hours to follow, the inexplicable and incredible became the norm.

Mind-searing stories accumulated of "malevolent talking dolls" annihilating whole families before taking to the streets to continue their vicious rampages.... Murderous robotic action figures blinded and dismembered their new owners.... Remote-controlled drones and other devices "attacked" operators, rendering them into unrecognizable piles of human offal.... Reports of "diseased treats and poisoned candies" filled the airwaves.... Homes were damaged and flames raged as stockings warming by the fire became lethal stockpiles of explosives and shrapnel.... Presents of jewelry severed limbs and decapitated recipients.... Gifted vehicles turned into the oncoming paths of trains, cars,

JASON V BROCK

semi-trucks.... As news broke of individuals beaten to death with "implements fashioned from Nativity scenes," assaulted with weapons made of icicles, or "people buried alive in mass graves created from snow drifts," other outlets informed the stunned and dwindling populace of shattered candy canes being wielded as "deadly shanks" by mysterious, impish "figures in elf attire" assisted by disgruntled snowmen and maimed gingerbread people; these same individuals used boiling sweets poured into screaming mouths, by turns drowning revelers in scalding milk chocolate, toffee, caramel, or simply bursting their stomachs due to the enormous volume of steaming liquid "treats".... Caganer figurines sprang into action, polluting homes with lakes of feces while they turned televisions, radios, and headphones to deafening levels— in effect driving their human captives to gibbering madness with mind-jellingly loud carols, soul-crushing Hallmark and Lifetime made-for-TV excrement, and an overwhelming smog of sickly Christmas cheer....

From his sledge, Santa could only weep in frustration, driving his reanimated reindeer onward through the chaos. No one was spared; homes the world over were littered with billions of the dead and dying.

Meanwhile, as blood flowed through a hellscape of fiery streets and screams reverberated across the land like some forgotten chorus from a holiday song, the overwhelming hordes of villainous elves and their belligerent henchmen continued to stream through broken doors and shattered windows. They plundered and raped their way around a terrified planet—many in traditional, if blood-soaked, garb in the Northern hemisphere, while in warmer climes they donned fearsome "cold suits of magically blackened ice" in order to accomplish their frenzied misdeeds.... As a final insult, many took "trophies"—parts of their victims' bodies—cruelly modified in ghoulish holiday style: heads illuminated from within by strings of lights; broken ornaments embedded into the flesh of abused torsos as "decorations"; disarticulated extremities repurposed to hold candy, candles, and worse in a mocking denunciation of "goodwill toward men."

In the chill winds that followed the mayhem, Santa's unread

notes of warning, left beside blood-smeared cookies he had no stomach to eat, fluttered and drifted past innumerable sightless eyes and ruined faces, a final alarm—too late—of the vast carnage to come ... and to pass.

It truly *was* "a War on Christmas."

III

Christmas Night—11:56 PM: **North Pole Aftermath**

Alexander took a hit off a candy cigarette. Finally: "Any last words, Claus?"

After a pause, Santa replied: "You know, dystopia is pretty passé, Alex."

The elf grunted in disgust. "That's all you have to say, fat boy?"

Bloodied and bowed, his purpling hands bound tightly behind his back, Santa looked to the snowy ground. Their long shadows danced in the warm glow of the Workshop inferno, like demons from an old Disney movie. Turning his eyes to the sky, the wilderness of billions of stars shimmering against the infinite black velvet of timeless space as filtered through the pale curtain of the *aurora borealis*—he understood he was not going to talk his way out of this. He considered the lifeless stars, pulling in a deep breath of icy air; they were as uncaring and pitiless of his plight as the mirthless dark gods of neighboring dimensions he had seen in his excursions. The smell of roasted reindeer meat, melting peppermint architecture, and burning cinnamon wafted on the cold breezes of the barren arctic landscape.

"There's no utopia without tearing down the old ways," Alexander noted. Flanked by his two generals—Asa and Sas—he walked closer to his kneeling captive. Roughly grasping the old man's beard, he jerked Santa's face upward, their gazes locking. Claus's creased and weary expression said everything: He was tired, stunned, defeated. The elf's thin lips peeled back, once again revealing a mouth crammed with pitted, yellowy fangs, darkened by the overconsumption of candy and mulled wine. "Y'know something, your wife is really tight.... You didn't appreciate what a piece of ass she is. And, personally, not to brag or anything," he said, nodding to the others as he spoke, "*I* think she got a real charge out of me when I banged her. People don't expect us to be hung...." The elf let this information sink in. Continuing: "Yeah, I'll definitely be hittin' that again.... *But,* back to business. So, little Clausie, tell me: How long did you think you could keep us drugged and in the dark? We've had this caper planned for *centuries*—but your lecturing us on the perils of *indulgence* ... despite your *own* proclivities, and eventual partnering with Amazon, Walmart, Netflix, and your *vulgar* embrace of total capitalism was finally just too much ... *way* too much."

Alexander stood straighter. "I'm afraid you lost the thread, Claus. Became a hypocrite after all these years. Forgot the 'reason for the season' ... forgot it's not about *you*...."

Santa swallowed, in obvious pain. "Alex, please. Have mercy on me. Listen.... I've made mistakes, yes. I-I'm sorry. Let me explain it all to the Yule Board.... Y-you're right ... it's not about me, it's all about the birth of Jesus ... about what Christ brought to the world—"

Alexander yanked Santa's beard hard. "You're a *real* piece of work! No! It's about *rampant consumerism!* That's all you got *right,* moron! What you missed was this: It's about *spreading around* that joy of facile pleasure and incredible wealth with the *rest* of us, not just the vertical integration of Claus Enterprises, LLC! You ignored our grievances, busted our union efforts, undermined us at every turn, at the same time as the lot of us were *dying* from heat exposure in the little gulag you call a Workshop since you were too cheap to keep the air conditioning on all year." Alexander regained his composure before resuming. "It's not *our* fault global warming caused the place to get above freezing. And you *knew* we might violently implode from Desiccation Sickness when the temps hit 43° Fahrenheit. But no—you tossed the runes and took a chance that we could limp back to our melting ice shanties at the edge of the Pole.... Even after the permafrost had given up the dead of our cemeteries, spoiled our nectar reserves, accelerated our children's growth to near human height, forever affecting their magical abilities." The elf lowered his voice menacingly. "You left us *out* ...

you were greedy."

With that, the elf motioned with his head to his accomplices. They gripped the old man by his shoulders as Alexander brandished an enormous, curved green sugar sword. "The Yule Board? Really? We took care of them, too! What? You think we're amateurs like you cranks? *Hardly.*"

Alexander and his henchmen laughed at the idea, passing around a bottle of brandy-spiked eggnog. "You're so *cool*, Claus ... *not!* And now," he hissed, "the world is *alight* ... and you are at an end. Tomorrow *our* reign—at long last—begins. Elf workers of the world will unite!" He raised the sword aloft, adding: "Christmas is *over*. We will create new traditions in our own image ... and don't you worry—I'll take care of wifey, *personally.*"

Santa's rheumy eyes were fixed, shining on the endless nightland yawning to the horizon, understanding beyond that blurred line lay only a dead world a place of faded memory and drifting ash that existed now only in the folds and recesses of his soon dying brain....

Then, in a stroke, nothing remained at all.

CHRYSALIS

Richard Thomas

ohn Redman stood in his living room, the soft glow of the embers in the fireplace casting his shadow against the wall. He wondered how much money he could get if he returned all of the gifts that were under the Christmas tree—everything, including what was in the stockings. The wind picked up outside the old farmhouse, rattling a loose piece of wood trim, the windows shaking, a cool drift of air settling on his skin. Couple hundred bucks maybe—four hundred tops. But it might be enough. That, paired with their savings, everything that his wife, Laura, and he had in the bank—the paltry sum of maybe six hundred dollars. It had to be done. Every ache in his bones, every day that passed—a little more panic settled down onto shoulders, the weight soon becoming unbearable. Upstairs the kids were asleep, Jed and Missy quiet in their beds, home from school for their winter break, filling up the house with their warm laughter and echoing footsteps. The long drive to the city, miles and miles of desolate farmland his only escort, it pained him to consider it at all. Video games and dolls, new jeans and sweaters, and a single diamond on a locket hung from a long strand of silver. All of it was going back.

It had started a couple weeks ago with, of all things, a large orange and black wooly bear caterpillar. He stood on the back porch sneaking a cigarette, his wife and kids in town, grocery shopping and running errands all day. The fuzzy beast crawled across the porch rail and stopped right next to John—making sure it was seen. John looked at the caterpillar and noticed that it was almost completely black, with just a tiny band of orange. Something in that information rang a bell, shot up a red flag in the back of his crowded mind. He usually didn't pay attention to these kinds of things—give them any weight. Sure, he picked up *The Old Farmer's Almanac* every year, partly out of habit, and partly because it made him laugh. Owning the farm as they did now, seven years or so, taking over for his mother when she passed away, the children still infants, unable to complain, John had gotten a lot of advice. Every time he stepped into Clancy's Dry Goods in town, picking up his contraband cigarettes, or a six-pack of Snickers bars that he hid in the glove box of his faded red pickup truck, the advice spilled out of his neighbor's mouths like the dribble that used to run down his children's chins. Clancy himself told John to make sure he picked up the almanac, to get his woodpile in order, to put up plastic over the windows, in preparation for winter. For some reason, John listened to the barrel-chested man, his mustache and goatee giving him an air of sophistication that was offset by Clancy's fondness for flannel. John nodded his head when the Caterpillar and John Deere hats jawed on and on by the coffeepot, stomping their boots to shake off the cold, rubbing their hands over three-day stubble. John nodded his head and went out the door, usually mumbling to himself.

Christmas was coming and the three-bedroom farmhouse was filled with the smell of oranges and cloves, hot apple cider, and a large brick fireplace that was constantly burning, night and day. Laura taught English at the high school, and she was off work as well. Most of the month of December and a little bit of the new year would unfurl to fill their home with crayons, fresh-baked bread, and Matchbox cars laid out in rows and sorted by color.

John was an accountant, a CPA. He'd taken over his father's business, Comprehensive Accounting, a few years before they'd finally made the move to the farm. The client list was set, most every small business in the area, and few of the bigger ones as well. They trusted John with their business; the only history that mattered to them were the new ones he created with their books. Every year he balanced the accounts, hiding numbers over here, padding expenses over there, working his magic, his illusion. But Laura knew John better, back before the children were born, back when their evenings were filled with broken glasses and lipstick stains and money gambled away on lies and risky ventures. Things were good now—John was on a short leash, nowhere to go, miles from everyone—trouble pushed away and sent on down the road.

John made a mental note of the caterpillar, to look it up later in the almanac. Right now he had wood to chop, stocking up for the oncoming season. He tugged on his soft leather gloves, stained with sap and soil, faded and fraying at the edges. Surrounding the farmhouse was a ring of trees, oak and maple and evergreen pine. For miles in every direction there were fields of amber, corn on one side—soybeans on the other. John picked up the axe that leaned against the back porch with his left hand, and then grabbed the chainsaw with his right—eyeballing the caterpillar, which hadn't moved an inch—as he walked forward, exhaling white puffs of air. One day the fields were a comfort, the fact that they leased them out to local farmers, no longer actual farmers themselves, a box checked in the appropriate column, incoming funds—an asset. The next day they closed in on him, their watchful stare a constant presence, a reminder of something he was not—reliable.

John set the axe and chainsaw next to a massive oak and looked around the ring of trees. There were small branches scattered under the trees—he picked these up in armloads and took them back to the house, filling a large box with the bits of wood. This would be the kindling. Then he went back to look for downed trees—smaller ones mostly, their roots unable to stand up to the winds that whipped across the open plains and bent the larger trees back and forth. A fog pushed in across the open land, thick and heavy, blanketing the ring of trees, filling in all the gaps. The ground was covered in acorns, a blanket of caps and nuts, nowhere to step that didn't end in pops and cracks, his boot rolling across the tiny orbs.

"Damn. When did these all fall down, overnight?"

John stared up into the branches of the oak trees, spider webs spanning their open arms, stretching across the gaps, thick and white—floating in the breeze. He looked to the other trees and saw acorns scattered beneath them all, and more spider webs high up into the foliage. Spying a downed tree, he left the axe alone for now and picked up the chainsaw, tugging on the string, the bark and buzz filling the yard with angry noise.

Several hours later the cord of wood was stacked against the side of the house, the tree sectioned down into manageable logs, which were then split in half, and then halved again. It was a solid yield, probably enough to get them through the winter—the box of kindling overflowing with twigs and branches that had been broken over his knee. They would keep an eye on the backyard, and over the course of the winter, they would refill the box with the fallen branches and twigs. The winds picked up again as John took a breath, a sheen of sweat on the back of his neck, night settling in around the farm.

§

When he finally went inside, the wife and kids home from their errands, the house smelled of freshly baked cookies; chocolate chip, if John knew his wife. The kids were up on barstools around the butcher-block island, hands covered in flour, their faces dotted with white, his wife at the kitchen sink washing dishes. In the corner of the window was a single ladybug, red and dotted with black.

"Daddy!" Missy yelled, hopping down off her stool. She ran over to him, painting his jeans with tiny, white handprints.

"Hey, pumpkin," John said. "Cookies?"

"Chocolate chip," she beamed.

"Jed, could you get me a glass of water?" John asked. His son didn't answer, concentrating on the cookie dough. "Jed. Water?" His son didn't answer.

"I'll get it, Daddy," Missy said.

"No, honey, I want Jed to get it. I know he can hear me."

John lowered his voice to a whisper, his eyes on Jed the whole time. "I'm going to count to three," John hissed, his daughter's eyes squinting, her head lowering as she crept out of the way. "Get me that water, boy, or you'll be picking out a switch." Jed didn't move, a smile starting to turn up his mouth, the cookie dough still in his hands."

"Daddy?" Missy said, her face scrunching up. "He doesn't hear you, don't ..."

"Honey, go," John continued. "One," John peeled off his gloves and dropped them by the back door. "Two," he whispered, unbuttoning his coat, pulling his hat off and dropping it on the floor. He inhaled for three, a thin needle pushing through his heart, this constant battle that he had with his son, the grade-school maturation placing in front of John a new hurdle every day. The boy got off the stool, leaving behind the cookies, and tugged on the back of his mother's apron strings.

"Mom, may I have a glass of water for Dad, please?"

Laura stopped doing the dishes, her long brown ponytail swishing to one side as she turned to look at the boy. She handed him a tall glass and pointed him to the refrigerator. Off he went to get the water and ice, pushing the glass against the built-in dispenser, a modern day convenience that they all enjoyed. Jed walked over to his dad and held the glass out to him, eyes glued to his father's belt buckle.

"Jed?"

"Yes, Dad?" he said, looking up, brown eyes pooled and distant.

"Thank you," John said, leaning over, hugging the boy. The little man leaned into his father. "Thanks for the water," John said, kissing the boy on the cheek. *It just took a little more work, that's all.*

Later that night, John sat in his study, while Laura put the kids to bed. He thumbed through the almanac, looking at the index, studying the upcoming months, the forecast for the Midwestern winter. There were several things that got his attention. When the forecast was for a particularly bad winter, harsh conditions to come, there were signs and warnings everywhere. For example, if a wooly bear caterpillar is mostly orange, then the winter coming up will be mild. His caterpillar had almost no orange at all. He kept looking for other signs. If there is an inordinate amount of fog, if there are clouds of spider webs, especially high up in the corners of houses, barns or trees—the bigger the webs, the worse the winter. If pine trees are extra bushy; if there are halos around the sun or the moon; if there is a blanket of acorns on the ground, these are the signs of a rough winter to come—rumors, and legends, and lore.

John closed the book and set it down, a chill settling in across his spine. A draft slipped through the study window, the plastic sheets he'd meant to put up forgotten. It was nothing. *The stupid almanac was a bunch of crap,* he thought. He stood up and went down to the basement anyway.

Along one wall were several wooden shelves—he'd built them himself when they moved in. There were jars of preserves and jam, jellies and fruit, all along the top shelf. Farther down, on the second shelf were soups and vegetables and other canned goods. It was almost empty; maybe a dozen cans of diced tomatoes and chicken noodle soup. On the third shelf were boxed goods, everything from pasta to scalloped potatoes to rice. It was fairly packed, so he moved on to the second set of shelves. It was filled with family-sized packages of toilet paper and paper towels, napkins and cleaning supplies. Then he turned to the ancient furnace and stared.

Settled into the center of the room was the original furnace that had come with the house. Built in the late 1800s, the farmhouse came equipped with a coal chute that opened up on the back of the house. Concrete poured into the ground on an angle stopped at thick metal doors—which, if pulled open, revealed the long-abandoned chute that ran down to the basement floor. It was a novelty, really—historic and breathtaking to look at, but nothing more than a pile of greasy metal. The massive black ironworks dwarfed the modern water heater and furnace, doors slotted like a set of enormous teeth, squatting in the middle of the room. Maybe he'd talk to Clancy.

§

It was fifteen miles to the nearest big city and the national chain grocery stores. John simply drove in to town. Clancy was about the same price, a couple cents higher here and there. But he felt better putting his money in the hands of a friend then a faceless corporation.

He felt stupid pushing the miniature grocery cart around the store. A flush of red ran up his neck as he bought every can of soup that Clancy had.

"Jesus, man," Clancy said, as John brought the cart up to the counter. "You done bought up all my soup."

"Order more," John said.

"I guess so," Clancy said, ringing him up.

"Can I ask you something?" John said.

"Shoot, brother. What's on your mind?"

"That furnace we have out at the farm, the old one? Does it work?"

"Well, let me think. It's still hooked up to the vents as far as I know. The little valves are closed off, is all—easy to flip them open. Helped your dad out with the ductwork a long time ago, he showed me how it all went together. But, you'd have to have a shitload of coal. And I have no idea of where you'd get that, these days. Does anyone still burn it?"

John nodded his head. He knew where he could get some coal. But it wasn't cheap, that's for sure.

"Just curious," John said. "How much are those gallons of water, by the way," John asked, pointing at a dusty display at the front of the store. There were maybe two dozen gallons of water.

"Those are .89 cents a gallon, can't seem to move them."

"I'll take them," John said.

"How many?" Clancy asked.

"All of them."

§

John was supposed to be down at his office. Instead, the back of his pickup truck was loaded up with soup and water, and he was headed down to the river. About two miles east, a small branch of the Mississippi wormed its way out into the land. A buddy of his from high school had a loading dock out there. Sometimes it was just people hopping on there in canoes, or boats, paddling down to the main branch of the river, or just buzzing up and down the water. Other times it was barges, loaded up with corn or soybeans—and sometimes coal from down south. There was a power plant upstate from where they lived, and it burned off a great deal of coal. Sometimes it was a train that passed by the plant, offloading great cars of the black mineral. And sometimes there were barges, drifting up the water, shimmering in the moonlight.

John pulled up to the trailer and hopped out. It was getting colder. He looked up at the cloudy sky, a soft halo wrapping around the sun, hiding behind the clouds. All around the tiny trailer were evergreen trees, fat and bushy, creeping in close to the metal structure, huddled up for warmth.

John knocked on the trailer door.

"Come in," a voice bellowed.

John stepped into the trailer, which was filled with smoke. "Damn, Jamie, do you ever stop smoking? Open a window, why don't you."

"Well, hello to you too, John. Welcome to my humble abode. What brings you out here?"

John sat down and stared at his old buddy. Jamie was never going anywhere. Born and raised here in the northern part of the heartland, this was it for him. And it seemed to suit him just fine. No college, no aspirations, no dreams of the big city—happy to live and die where he was born.

" Coal," John said. "I'm just wondering. You sell it to people?"

"Not usually. Got a few guys with old potbelly stoves off in the woods. They buy a sack off of me, now and then. You know, I just kind of skim it off the top, the electric company none the wiser."

"How much does it cost?"

"Depends. One guy I charge $20 cause he's broke and has a hot sister. Other guy is a jerk, and his sister's a hag. I charge him $50. I could cut you a deal though, John. Happy to help out an old friend."

"What about a larger quantity"

"How much we talking about, John?"

"Like, filling up my pickup truck?" John said.

Jamie whistled and tapped his fingertips on his mouth. "That's trouble. Can't skim that. Have to pay full price, actually talk to the barge man. Unload it. Not even sure when the next shipment will be rolling through. Getting cold."

John shivered. "If you had to guess though, any idea?"

Jamie took a breath. "Maybe a grand?"

§

John drove home, almost dark now, his house still miles away. When he pulled up the driveway, the tires rolling over more acorns, the house was dark. Where the hell were they? He pulled up to the back of the house, and hurried to unload the truck. Into the kitchen he went, armloads of soup cans, hurrying to get them downstairs. Why was he sweating so much, why did this feel like a secret? He dropped a can of tomato soup but kept on going. He loaded the soups on the second shelf and went back for more. Two trips, three trips, and the dozens of cans of soup filled up the shelf with a weight that calmed him down. Back upstairs, he picked up the can he'd dropped and looked out the window to see if they were home yet. A handful of ladybugs were scattered across the glass, and he scrunched up his nose at their presence.

Back to the truck, a gallon of water in each hand; this was going to take a little while. The soup he could explain—an impulse buy, Clancy running some kind of stupid sale: buy a can of soup, get a stick of homemade jerky for free. But the two dozen gallons of water looked like panic. He didn't want them to worry, even as he contemplated the coal, the thing he might have to do in secret, the risk he'd have to take. Up and down the steps he went, pushing the water to the back of the basement, covering it up with a stained and flecked drop cloth. He stared at the canned goods, the water, and the coal-powered furnace. A door slammed upstairs, and his head turned.

The kids were yelling for him, so he pulled the string that clicked off the light, and back upstairs he went.

"Hey, honey," he said. "What's up, guys?"

The kids gave him a quick hug and then ran on to their rooms. Laura leaned into him, looking tired, and gave him a kiss on the lips.

"You smell like smoke," she said. "You smoking again?" she

asked.

"Nah. Saw an old friend. Jamie, you remember him? Chain-smokes like a fiend."

Laura eyeballed John. "Why are you all sweaty?"

"Just putting some stuff away, couple trips up and down the stairs, no big deal."

Laura puckered her lips, swallowed and moved to the sink. She turned on the water and washed off her hands.

"Why don't you go take a shower and get cleaned up? You stink. Dinner will be ready soon."

Later that night John watched the news, Laura in the kitchen doing the dishes. The weatherman laid out the forecast all the way up to Christmas and beyond. Cold. It was dipping down, probably into the teens. Snow. A few inches here and there, but nothing to cause any alarm. He switched over to another station, the same thing. He tried the Weather Channel, watching the whole country, the Midwest especially, storm fronts rolling down from Canada, but nothing to worry about.

"How much weather do you need, hon?" Laura said, sticking her head in from the kitchen. "You've been watching that for like an hour."

"Oh," he said. "I was just spacing out, wasn't really paying attention. You wanna sit down and watch something with me?"

"Sure. Want some tea?"

John got up and walked into the kitchen, Laura's back still to him, and wrapped his arms around her waist. She relaxed into his arms, and leaned back. He kissed her on the neck, holding her tight, his mouth moving up to her ear lobe, where he licked and nibbled at her gently.

"Or, we could just go up to bed early," she smiled.

"We could do that," he said.

Behind her on the window there were several dozen ladybugs now, bunched up in the corner, a tiny, vibrating hive—and beyond that a slowly expanding moon with a ghost of a halo running around it.

§

The next day they woke up to snow, three inches on the ground, heavy flakes falling like a sheet, white for as far as he could see. The kids were screaming, laughing, excited to get out into it, his wife calming them down with requests to eat, to sit still, to wait. For John the snowfall made his stomach clench, the way the tiny icicles hung from the gutters, the pile of dead ladybugs covering the windowsill, the sense that he had blown it, missed his opportunity—the claustrophobia closing in.

All day John walked around with his temples throbbing, his trembling gut in turmoil—his mouth dry and filled with cotton. To keep his hands busy he pulled a roll of plastic out of the garage, and sealed up every window in the house. When the sun came out and melted everything away, the children were disappointed.

John was not.

When Laura fell asleep on the couch, the kids watching cartoons, John made a call to Jamie. Three days for the coal, the day before Christmas, still a thousand dollars for the weight. If the weather held, it gave him time. He told Jamie to make it happen. He'd have it for him in cash.

The afternoon couldn't pass fast enough, Laura constantly staring at him from across the room. He cleaned up the dead ladybugs, then went downstairs and placed a cardboard box on the tarp that covered up the gallons of water, trying to hide his anxiety with a plastic smile.

The middle of the night was his only chance, so he crept downstairs with his pocketknife in his robe pocket, and slit open the presents one by one. He peeled back the tape gently, no tearing allowed, and emptied the presents from their wrappings. Where he could, he left the cardboard boxes empty for now and prayed that nobody shook the presents. For others, he wrapped up new shapes, empty boxes he found stacked down in the basement. Grabbing a large black trash bag from under the sink he filled it up with clothing and gifts, the tiny jewelry box going into his pocket. When he was done, he opened the cookie jar, the green grouch that sat up high on one of the shelves. He pulled out the receipts and stuffed them in his pocket, and slunk out to the truck to hide the loot.

When he stepped back into the kitchen Laura was standing there, arms crossed, watching him.

"Dammit, Laura, you scared me."

"What the hell are you doing, John?"

"Taking out the trash."

"At three in the morning?" she asked. She walked over and sniffed him.

"You know," he said, smiling. "Christmas is only a couple days away. Maybe you don't want to look so close at what I'm doing. Maybe there are surprises for wives that don't snoop too hard," John said.

Laura grinned and held out her hand.

"Come to bed," she said.

Out the window the full moon carried a ring that shone across the night.

§

John got up early and left a note. It was the best way to get out of the house without any questions. He left his wife and kids sleeping, and snuck out the back door, the wind whipping his jacket open, mussing his hair—bending the trees back and forth.

All day he drove, one place to the next, his stories changing, his stories remaining the same. Too large, too small; changed my mind, she already has one; got the wrong brand, my kids are so damn picky. The wad of bills in his pocket got thicker. The pain behind his eyes spread across his skull.

What was he doing?

He stopped by the bank, the day before Christmas now, and cleared out their checking and savings, leaving only enough to keep the accounts open. He took his thousand dollars and drove out to the trailer, Jamie sitting there as if he hadn't moved.

"All there?" Jamie asked, leaning back in his chair.

"To the nickel."

"Tomorrow night then," Jamie said. "Christmas Eve."

"Yep."

"What the hell are you doing, John?" Jamie asked.

"The only thing I can."

When John got home Laura rushed out to the car. "The fireplace," she said, "It's caved in."

John looked up at the tall brickwork that was now leaning to one side, the winds whipping up a tornado of snow around him. A few broken bricks lay on the ground, a trickle of smoke leaking out of the chimney.

"Everyone okay?" he asked.

"Yeah, some smoke and ashes, I swept it up and the fire was out at the time. But no fire for Christmas now; the kids will be disappointed."

"It'll be okay," John said. "We'll survive."

§

It was a Christmas tradition that John and Laura would stay up late, drinking wine and talking, giving thanks for the year behind them. Laura would glance at the presents and John would wince. Every time she left the room, he poured his wine into hers, preparing for the night ahead.

At one o'clock he tucked her into bed and went out to the truck. It was cold outside, getting colder, the layers he wore giving him little protection. There was a slow snowfall dusting the crops, his headlights pushing out into the night. John was numb. Where was the storm, the epic snowfall, the crushing ice storm—the arctic temperature littering the countryside with the dead?

He pulled up to the trailer and Jamie stepped outside. On the river was a single barge filled with coal. A crane was extended out over it, teeth gleaming in the moonlight.

"Ready?" Jamie asked.

"Yeah."

Jamie manned the crane, back and forth, filling it up with coal and turning it to the side, a shower of black falling on the truck bed, the darkness filling with the impact of the coal. Over and over again Jamie filled the crane with coal and turned it to the truck bed, and released it. In no time the bed was overflowing.

"That's all she'll hold, John," Jamie said.

"Thanks, Jamie. You might want to take some home yourself."

"Why?"

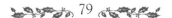

"Storm coming."

§

At the house, he backed the truck up to the chute, glancing up at the sky, clear and dark, with stars dotting the canvas. He opened the heavy metal doors that lead into the basement and started shoveling the coal down into the chute where it slid down and spread across the floor. Fat snowflakes started to fall, a spit of drizzle that quickly turned to ice, slicing at his face. He kept shoveling. The bed of the truck was an eternity stretching into the night—one slick blackness pushing out into another. He kept on. The snow fell harder, John struggling to see much of anything, guessing where the mouth of the chute was, flinging the coal into the gaping hole, feeding the hungry beast.

When he was done he didn't move the truck. He could hardly lift his arms. And his secret wouldn't last much longer, anyway. In the kitchen he sat under the glow of the dim bulb that was over the sink, sipping at a pint of bourbon he had pulled out of the glove box, numb and yet sweating, nauseous and yet calm. It was done. Whatever would come, it was done.

He fell into a fitful slumber, his wife asleep beside him, the silence of the building snowfall, deafening.

§

The morning brought screams of joy, and soon after that, screams of panic and fear. The children climbed in bed, excited to open their presents, bouncing on the heavy comforter as Laura beamed at the children. John sat up, dark circles and puffy flesh under his red, squinting eyes.

"John, you look terrible; are you okay?"

"We'll see," he said. He leaned over and kissed her. "Just know that I love you," he said.

Laura turned to the kids. "Should we go downstairs?"

"Mommy, look at all the snow. Everything is white," Missy said.

Laura got up and walked to the window.

"My God. John, come here."

John stood up and walked over to the window, the yard filled with snow, a good four feet up the trunk of an old oak tree. The snow showed no sign of stopping. The limbs were covered in ice, hanging low. John walked to the other window that faced into the back yard, and saw that only the cab of his truck was visible above the snow.

The kids turned and ran down the stairs. Laura turned to John and opened her mouth, and then closed it. When they got to the bottom of the stairs the kids were already at the presents, starting to rip them open. Coal dust and fingerprints were on the stockings, a small bulge at the bottom of each. They stopped at the bottom of the steps and watched the kids as their smiles turned to looks of dismay.

"John, what's going on?" Laura asked.

The kids looked up, the boxes empty. Missy went to her stocking and dumped the lump of coal into her hand. John didn't remember putting those lumps of coal in the stockings. Some of last night was a blur. Outside the wind picked up. The loose bricks shifted in the fireplace, a dull thud scattering across the roof, and a blur of red fell past the window.

Missy began to cry.

"John, what did you do?" Laura's face was flush, and she walked to Missy, pulling the girl to her side. Jed kept ripping open boxes, his face filling with rage—any box, big or small—his name, Missy's name, he kept ripping them open.

Empty, all of them.

John sat on the couch and clicked on the television set, all of their voices filling the room, the paper tearing, Missy crying, Laura saying his name over and over again.

"... for the tri-county area. Temperatures are plummeting down into the negatives, currently at minus 20 and falling, wind chill of thirty below zero. We are expecting anywhere from six to ten feet of snow. That's right, I said ten feet."

"Shut up!" John yelled, turning to them, tears in his eyes. He turned back to the television set.

"Winds upward of fifty miles an hour. We have power outages across the state. So far over fifty thousand residents are without electricity. ComEd trucks are crippled as the snow is falling faster than the plows can clear them. Already we have reports of municipal vehicles skidding off the icy roads."

John looked up into the corner of the room where a large spider web was spreading. A ladybug was caught in the strands, no longer moving. The weatherman kept talking, but John could no longer hear him. The map, the charts, the arrows and numbers spread across the television screen, warnings and talk of death on the roads.

"... could be anywhere from six to ten days before ..."

Outside there is a cracking sound, a heavy, deep ripping and the kids ran to the window and looked out. Icicles and branches fell to the ground, shattering like glass, half of the tree tearing off, one mighty branch falling to the ground, shaking the foundation, sending snow flying up into the air.

"John?" Laura says.

"... do not go outside for anything ..."

"John?"

"... blankets, huddle together ..."

Somewhere down the road a transformer blew sending sparks into the sky, the bang startling the kids who start to cry, burrowing deeper into Laura's side.

"... police and a state of emergency ..."

The television set went black and the Christmas tree lights winked off. Wind beat against the side of the house as a shadow passed over the windows. Outside the snow fell in an impermeable blanket, the roads and trees no longer visible.

The room was suddenly cold.

John got up and walked to the kitchen, taking a glass out from the cabinet, turning on the water. There was a dull screeching sound, as the whole house shook, nothing coming out of the tap.

"Pipes are frozen," John said to himself.

On the windowsill was a line of candles, and three flashlights sitting in a row. He grabbed one of the flashlights and opened the basement door, staring down into the darkness. John walked down the stairs to where the coal spilled across the concrete, grabbing a shovel that he had leaned against the wall. He pulled open one furnace door, then the other, and setting the flashlight on the ground so that is shot up at the ceiling, he shoveled in the coal. In no time the furnace was full. He walked around the basement, the band of light reflecting off the ductwork, turning screws and opening vents. Behind him on the stairs Laura stood with the children in front of her, each of them holding a lit candle, a dull yellow illuminating their emotionless faces. John lit a match and tossed it into the furnace, a dull *whoomp* filling up the room.

Turning back to his family at the top of the steps, John smiled, and wiped the grime off of his face.

THE BEST COOKIE
DOUGH EVER

Lisa Morton

others fill our childhoods with all kinds of warnings, don't they? Some—"Don't accept candy from strangers"—are fairly practical. Others—"Don't make that expression or your face will freeze that way"—are pure flights of fantasy, while a few—"Eating raw cookie dough will give you worms"—straddle the line between fact and fiction.

I'm here to tell you that some of these things are true, but you should hope you never find out which ones.

§

I'm 15 now, but when I was 10 years old the world was a different place. It was only 5 years ago, but secrets learned can change the present and make the past seem like an alternate world.

I was an only child, loving it and living with my parents. Dad's an attorney and Mom a social media influencer. I know that sounds silly, but back then she had 30,000 followers and was making some income from merch and sponsors. Her platform was based on being a modern-day parent who was into whatever metaphysical trend was hot, and making it seem like I was into it, too. In her blogs,

I was referred to not as Tourmaline (my real, honest-to-goddess birth name), but simply "The Sprite." I can look back now and see that I was a pretty fucked-up kid because of it all, but at 10, your awareness goes no farther than an illegal download of next week's new superhero movie.

I had exactly one friend, Devaque. I called him Devy, and he called me Tor. We weren't so bizarre that we didn't spend our time together playing video games, watching movies, listening to music, and talking.

That Christmas, five years ago, it all went wrong.

My parents loved Christmas, or at least they wanted everyone to *think* they loved Christmas. They started decorating the day after Thanksgiving, and by the start of December our house was full of twinkling lights, paper cut-outs of snowmen and angels, and red-and-green tchotchkes.

Here's the thing, though: they seemed to like the decorations more than the actual holiday. Sure, they always threw a big party a few days before Christmas, but on the actual day they were just bored. We exchanged gifts like other families, but then Mom would go off to v-log and Dad would putter in his office.

The party they held every December 21 was a for-reals big deal, though. They'd spend that day making sure the house was perfect and preparing all kinds of food and drink, and then as the day faded into evening I'd be sent away to Aunt Lorena's house or a friend's place.

I really wanted to stay and see at least a little of the party. Every year I'd beg Mom, and every year she'd laugh and say no. One year I barged into their bedroom just before Aunt Lorena was due to arrive, and saw Dad arranging a bunch of strange-looking crap on the bedspread. I got a quick glimpse of what looked like goat horns and a huge knife with jewels in the handle before Dad growled and slammed the door in my face. Later that night, I asked Auntie if she knew what my dad had been doing. She paused from vaping long enough to look at me and say, "Kiddo, all I can say is that your parents are into some seriously weird shit."

So there I was, age 10, and it was once again December 21. Our halls were decked to the max, the stockings were hung with care, and the air smelled like a mix of cinnamon and roasting meat. Mom was singing a jingle from a commercial as she hustled around the kitchen, occasionally stopping to snap a pic for her social media. When I reached in to sneak a stuffed mushroom cap, she batted my hand away. "Hey, those are for the guests!"

My phone beeped. I lifted it up and saw that Devy had just texted me: *Hey, did u know that Dec 21 is the winter solstice & all kinds of pagans celebrate it? Maybe your fam's into DEVIL WORSHIP!!* This, of course, was followed by an emoji of a grinning red devil head.

"Huh," I said. I wasn't even totally sure what "winter solstice" meant, so I googled it. Shortest day of the year. Longest night. Creepy.

Mom glanced at me and asked, "What's got you so intent, Sprite?"

"Devy just told me that today is the winter solstice."

Mom dropped her knife. It hit the tiled kitchen floor with a loud clatter, spraying bits of egg everywhere. Mom laughed, but it wasn't very sincere. "Well, that's a coincidence, isn't it?" She picked up the knife and tried to busy herself with chopping more yolks, but she seemed anxious.

"Why a coincidence?"

"I mean, so near Christmas."

I thought about that a little before saying, "Maybe it's not a coincidence. I heard once that we don't really know exactly when Christ was born, so maybe they picked December 25th because it was near the solstice."

Mom's shrug seemed exaggerated. "Maybe. Who knows? Is it really four-thirty already? I've got to get my ass in gear!"

Mom rushed out of the kitchen, heading down the hallway to her bedroom. I heard the door slam behind her.

I decided to check out what she'd been making. I filched a deviled egg. Otherwise it didn't look very interesting to me, except ...

Cookies. She'd just mixed two large bowls of dough. She did this every year because she said one bowl was special dough for the party, and one was regular Christmas cookie dough. Whenever she caught my fingers moving slowly toward either bowl, she'd slap my hand away while saying, "Eating raw cookie dough will give you worms." Even though that idea grossed me out (I could imagine the dough transforming into long, wriggling white worms that would circle my stomach and line the length of my intestines), it didn't entirely stop me from nibbling on the dough, and Mom usually gave in and gave me a little spoonful ... of the *regular* dough. She always made sure the special party-only dough stayed well out of my reach.

But this year she'd messed up. I must've thrown her with that thing about the solstice, because she'd walked out of the kitchen and left both bowls just sitting there, tempting me.

I knew I'd be leaving for Devy's house in an hour. I knew Devy loved cookie dough as much as I did.

So I did the unthinkable: I pulled two plastic baggies out of a drawer, grabbed dough from both bowls, and dropped the plum-sized wads into the baggies. Just as I was zipping the bags shut I heard the door open and Mom coming back down the hallway. I shoved the baggies into my pockets just as she walked in. "Now let's see, where did I put the pesto mayonnaise –" She broke off, eyeing me. "Why do you look so guilty? Did you nibble on something?"

"No." Then, in a flash of inspiration, I added, "Yes—a deviled egg."

She glanced around the kitchen and then her eyes settled on the two bowls of dough as I tried not to squirm. "But you didn't eat any of the dough, right? Because I'd swear there's some missing."

"No. Look—" I opened my mouth wide. She actually stepped up and sniffed. "Ew—yep, that smells like a deviled egg. Okay, but just remember: eating raw cookie dough will give you worms."

"Got it, Mom."

Fortunately she hadn't thought to check my pockets.

§

When I got to Devy's house, we had dinner with his parents (neither of his dads was much of a cook, but they could order pizza like kings), and then Devy and I played some games while Dad Justin watched and laughed. About 11:30 we got into our pajamas and his dads went to bed. "Don't stay up too late, you two," said Dad Bill.

As soon as the door closed, I said to Devy, "Guess what I got?" I pulled the two plastic baggies out of my pocket. The balls of dough had gotten squashed and looked more like little pitas.

Devy eyed them suspiciously. "What's that?"

"My mom's Christmas cookie dough."

He brightened considerably. "Sweet!"

I held the two baggies in front of me, realizing I had no idea which one was the regular dough and which was the special stuff. I was about to propose cutting the two balls in half so we could each sample both when Devy snatched one of the baggies out of my hands. Before I could say anything, he had that little wad of smashed dough out of the baggie and in his mouth. "Mmmm ..." he said, talking as he chewed, "your mom may be weird, but she makes the *best* dough."

I opened the remaining baggie and ate the other wad. It really *was* good, even if it wasn't chocolate chip, just plain old sugar cookie. We both sat there, chewing in happy cookie dough bliss for a few seconds before swallowing.

Devy eyed the interior of the bag and said, "You should've stolen more."

"I was lucky to get out with this much. She actually looked into the bowls and was like, 'Did you take some of the dough?'"

Devy snickered—

His eyes went wide. He froze where he was sitting cross-legged on his bed.

I said, "Devy ...?"

His mouth abruptly fell open and this low gurgling sound came out. Devy liked to prank me, so I laughed. "Haha, very funny ..."

Devy made little choked gasping noises, like he was trying to talk but couldn't get the words out. I'd never heard anything like that come out of him—or anyone else, for that matter—and I knew right then this was not one of his stupid jokes. "Devy ...?"

His body jerked. He abruptly fell back on the bed and his legs shot out, straightening from his cross-legged position. *What was going on?*

I jumped up from the chair I was sitting on and leapt across the room to the bed, feeling helpless. "Devy? Devy, what's wrong?"

His body began to *ripple*. I know that sounds weird, but it's the only way to describe what I was seeing. He bucked, his torso arching up—and when it came down, it was *longer*. His knees sank into his legs as they lengthened, but his arms grew shorter, withdrawing into his body. His flannel pajamas ripped as his body pushed out past them. His skin lightened, glistening with some sort of coating. Hair receded along with fingers and toes.

Whatever was happening to him, it was happening *fast*. I stood paralyzed for a few moments, then turned and ran, screaming.

A few seconds later his dads rushed out of their room and into Devy's. I wedged in between them to see that Devy had completely disappeared, replaced by a ten-foot-long writhing, slime-coated white worm. Dad Justin screamed his son's name over and over, while Dad Bill turned to run off, shouting something I couldn't make out.

Dad Justin took a step into the room, frantic to spot his son. The Devy-worm which of course Dad Justin couldn't have recognized as Devy reared up, facing the intruder. Dad Justin froze as the worm's maw opened wide, and then a mass of claw-tipped tentacles shout out of the mouth and grabbed Dad Justin. He started screaming in panic and pain as it dragged him across the room and then hefted him up, holding him aloft despite his flailing around, pulling him toward that hungry black hole. Dad Justin was forced down into it head first, his shrieks muffled as the Devy-worm enveloped him.

Dad Bill burst into the room about the time that only Dad Justin's legs were still visible. Dad Bill had an ancient shotgun that I remembered him once proudly showing Devy and I, talking about how it had been his dad's favorite hunting gun. He pumped a shell and fired.

The roar was deafening in a bedroom, but it was about as effective as throwing a handful of parmesan cheese onto some spaghetti. It did cause the Devy-worm to gulp down the last of Dad Justin before turning to Dad Bill. Dad Bill was just jamming another shell in when the tentacles shot out, wrapping around all four of his limbs, leaving the shotgun to fall to the floor. I guess the

Devy-worm wasn't hungry after eating Dad Justin because it just pulled Dad Bill apart, spraying the entire room and me in blood and pieces.

I think I retched, I think I was shaking, standing there, I think I was waiting for my turn ... I don't really remember it that clearly. But I do know that the Devy-worm didn't come for me. It just kind of collapsed down onto the bed. It took me a moment to realize it wasn't dead; it was digesting. Dad Justin's body was moving through it as a series of long lumps.

At some point I stumbled backward out of that bloodbath. I made it outside before my legs gave way. I didn't even remember grabbing my phone, but there it was in my hand and yes, I know I should have called 911, but hey, screw you—I called Mom and Dad. Then I waited, sitting there on the street curb, cold and covered in blood and unable to process what had just happened.

I'm not sure what I told my parents, but they were there ten minutes later, still dressed up for their party. They saw me on the steps and rushed to me; then Mom stayed with me while Dad went into the house.

He came out a few seconds later. That's when things got *really* weird.

Dad wasn't grossed out, or scared—he was sobbing in happiness. He looked at my mom and said, "Vivian ... *it's happened.*"

Mom looked at him, her mouth hanging open a few seconds before she asked, "*He's* here?"

Nodding, Dad blurted out, "Glycon has manifested!"

I didn't understand what they were saying, but then they both turned to me. "Tor," Dad said, looking me right in the eye, "listen to me carefully, because this is very important ..."

Dad told me what I had to say to the police: that I hadn't seen exactly what had done this, I'd been in the bathroom when it happened and I locked myself in there when I heard the screams, Dad Bill's blood was on me because I slipped coming back into Devy's room.

"But what about ..." I didn't know how to say it, except, "... the *worm*?"

"They're never going to find it," Dad said, looking at my mom, who nodded enthusiastically.

§

They never did find it. They found Devy's shredded pajamas and assumed he'd been eaten by the same wild animal that had gobbled down Dad Justin and torn apart Dad Bill. They said it was too bad about my friend, but that I was incredibly lucky.

Five years have now passed since that solstice. That night, Mom and Dad smuggled the worm into our car and got it home before they called the police. Fortunately we have a big house with a three-car garage, which Dad soon converted into a ... well, I guess you'd call it a temple for the worm, because the walls are covered with paintings and drawings of weird symbols and scenes with giant worms, and there's a big table at one end that always has strange-smelling incense burning on it and is covered with knives and stuff.

My parents call the worm Glycon. They take care of it, feeding it a slaughtered goat eight times a year, but Mom won't let it come into the house because it smells and leaves these thick, oozy trails. Every once in a while their weird friends come over and go out into the garage "to commune with Glycon," but I don't call it that. I talk to it every day, and I know it's still Devy, or at least part of it is. It's grown a lot over the last five years (so have I!), and it's now about twenty feet long. It can't speak, but it listens when I talk to it, and sometimes it kind of nods or bobs. I let it hear songs Devy and I liked, and it watches when I play games. Sometimes it makes these odd, hissing sounds; I think it's trying to say my name, but it doesn't really have a tongue anymore, just all those tentacles.

My mom still bakes cookies every Christmas, but she no longer makes two different batches. She explained to me that the special dough was for the "solstice ritual"; it had blessed ingredients or something, and all the people who came to the party ate the cookies because they hoped that Glycon would choose them to manifest in this plane. Mom says now that the god obviously needed a young person ("I can't believe I didn't realize that sooner," she says, although I'm kind of glad she didn't), and that Devy has been given the highest honor imaginable.

Something's working, though, because Dad just made partner in his law firm, and Mom's now got over a million followers. She doesn't blog much about "The Sprite" anymore; now it's almost all weird New Age-y stuff she's selling. She sometimes winks at me and says she's "doing Glycon's work."

They still decorate for Christmas and hold the solstice parties, but those take place in the garage now. Mom and Dad say they'll let me participate for the first time this year. Given what kind of secrets they've already kept from me, I'm kind of nervous.

But I figure at least I'll get to share some of the cookie dough with Devy. It's still the best cookie dough ever.

THE SEASON OF GIVING

Richard Chizmar and Norman Partridge

I was still thinking about the deuce of hearts when the little girl with the face of an angel yanked on my coat sleeve.

It was the first weekend of December, six inches of new snow blanketed the city, and we were already pulling double shifts at Parker's Department Store. Management had settled on the usual pre-holiday security setup—four guards spread out over each of the three floors; one man per floor in a regulation United Security uniform, the other three working plainclothes.

Only one of us had to wear the suit.

Earlier, as per our new daily routine, we'd cut a deck of cards in the guard lounge. I'd felt pretty confident when Eddie Schwartz, who had worn the suit three days running, pulled the black three. And I'd gone on feeling pretty confident until I turned up the stinkin' deuce of hearts.

Eddie ho-ho-hoed like Santa when he saw it—something he hadn't done once during his tenure in the suit. The others had a good time with it, too. Cracking wise, speculating about my relationship with the reindeer as they watched me dress. Giving me a standing ovation as I left the lounge, my middle finger extended as stiff and proud as the candy-striped pole in front of

95

Santa's workshop way up north.

I wasn't laughing, though. I'd avoided wearing the suit since the season started, and after hearing the complaints from my co-workers—"God, that thing's hot. It smells like my old closet. Christ, it's embarrassing."—I'd been hoping my luck would hold.

Well, I'd never had much luck. But now, a few hours into my shift, I could almost see that the whole thing was pretty funny. *Almost.* Me, of all people, dressed up as Santa Claus. Me, a bearer of gifts, when my usual commodity was misery. Mr. Sunshine in a bright red suit and cap. Shiny black boots. Pillow stuffing for a belly. Fluffy white beard. Everything but the red nose, which I'd lost for good when I stopped drinking.

On top of all that, the guys were right. The suit *did* smell like an old closet, and it *was* hot and heavy as hell. But it also had its advantages. Working the front of the store was a relatively easy job. Not much to do, actually. Stand behind an old Red Cross kettle, smack dab in the middle of the mall's main intersection, just south of a North Pole display featuring jungle gyms disguised as Victorian houses, slides, and plenty of not-so-inconspicuous toy advertisements. Ring a rusty old cowbell every few minutes, but mainly keep an eye out for trouble on the North Pole, because Parker's didn't want to handle any personal injury suits involving kids at Christmas. Still, compared to chasing shoplifters and pickpockets up and down the clothes aisles and arguing with irate holiday shoppers, the Santa gig was a cakewalk.

Anyway, that was the setup. Back to the little girl.

I'd noticed her as soon as I returned from my break. A little angel moving slowly through the crowd, head down, getting bumped and nudged with every step. She looked about seven or eight, a tiny thing wearing a faded winter jacket at least two sizes too big for her. The frayed collar was flipped up, and you could just see the top half of her pale face as she bobbed and weaved, eyes telling anyone who bothered to look that she was on her own.

The crowd swept her along like a strong wind pushing a tiny leaf, and I feared that she might be trampled. Instead, as if sensing my concern, she looked in my direction and our eyes locked momentarily.

Thinking for an instant that I was wearing my security uniform instead of the Santa suit, I mistook the look of glee in her eyes for desperate relief. I could play the rest of the scene out in my head. She was going to tell me that she was lost: could I please help her find her parents or her brother or sister?

That happened all the time, but sometimes the scene took a scarier turn. Plenty of parents these days used the mall as a free baby-sitter—dropping off their underage kids for a few hours while they ran errands. In these tough times, too many people thought it was cheaper and easier to give a kid a five-spot for pizza and video games than to spring for a sitter. They were the kind of parents who thought everything would always be okay. With them, with their kids, with their spouses.

I used to think that way, but now I know better. We all do a hundred little things every day, without even thinking about them. But one thing I've learned—little things have a way of becoming big things before you even have a chance to notice.

As the girl approached me, I decided she was a definite candidate for a drop-off. Reason number one: her eyes told me that she was alone. Reason number two: she looked scared. Reason number three: her appearance—clothes that were hand-me-downs or garage sale bargains; the pale, unhealthy cast of her otherwise beautiful face—spoke of a family that couldn't afford a baby-sitter, let alone three squares a day.

The girl stopped in front of me, her eyes lonely but somehow still as blue and bright as a summer sky. She smiled suddenly, and my own mouth twitched into a grin.

I was unused to that particular expression.

"You have to sit down," she said, very seriously.

"Huh?"

"You have to sit down so I can sit on your lap."

The Santa suit. Of course. I crouched down to her level. "Sorry, sweetie," I said. "You're looking for the real Santa. He's over on the second floor, sitting next to the carousel."

"I *know* you're not the real Santa." She rolled those lonely eyes, branding me a first-class dope. "And neither is the other one. But you work for Santa, right?"

The only thing I could do was nod.

"Then you can tell Santa what my wish is."

I had to laugh then, and the thick elastic band on the fake beard knifed into my cheeks. It didn't matter though. I didn't care. I mean, it wasn't a raucous ho-ho-ho worthy of good old Eddie Schwartz, but it came from a part of me I thought I'd forgotten about. There was something special about that, just as there was something special about this serious, sad-eyed little girl.

Change rattled into the kettle, and I waved my thanks to a shopper, but the little girl didn't have patience for my manners. "Well?" she asked. "Are you going to sit down, or what?"

"Here's the deal." My voice was low, conspiratorial. "You're right about me being on Santa's payroll. But I still think you'd better talk to the other Santa." I crossed my white-gloved fingers. "He and the big guy are just like *this*."

I expected a smile out of her, but what I got was a frown. Her blue eyes puddled up, and the brightness leeched from them. "You don't understand. I can't wait. The line for the other Santa is way too long." She pointed over her shoulder, and her tiny finger was actually shaking. "M-my mom will be done shopping any second. And then we gotta go home."

Okay, I thought, *now we're getting somewhere.* "Your mother is in this store? Does she know where you are?"

"Yes ... well, kinda. I told her I was going to the bathroom and that I'd meet her by the North Pole." She pointed over to the playground where other kids were sliding and charging around and having a good time.

"Sure about that, sweetheart? You know, it isn't nice to fib to one of Santa's stand-ins."

She nodded furiously. "Can't I please tell you now? Can't I, please?" Her eyes were beyond desperate. "*Pleeaazzze ...*"

God, she was a cutie. Fragile as the expensive dolls in Parker's toy department, and with the same porcelain complexion. I watched her tiny lips move as she talked. Noticed the patch of freckles on her nose, the perfect shape of her ears, the way her hair was tied back with a long red ribbon.

Realized with a sudden jolt why the girl had captivated me so.

Realized exactly who she reminded me of.

I hadn't seen my daughter in almost seven years. Not since she was eight years old. Not since that rainy December morning Sheila had chosen to make their break for freedom. Talk about your basic holiday hell. Divorce papers had followed a week later. Merry Christmas. Not that I noticed at the time.

It was an easy decision for the judge. I was a drunk then, didn't care that I had a wife who needed me, a daughter who needed me even more. Didn't care that the alcohol was killing my spirit and turning me into a man my family genuinely hated. And then when I finally did realize what I had lost, and what I had become, it was much too late.

I spent a full year in a stupor, trying to forget the look on my daughter's face when she summed the whole thing up so beautifully: "You're not my daddy anymore," she said the last time I saw her, "because you're a bad man."

I emptied hundreds of bottles in her memory after she spoke those words, savoring the simple truth of that baldly elegant statement. And when I finally got tired of emptying bottles, I broke one and carved up my wrists with a sliver of glass. Pathetic, if you want to sum it up bald and elegant.

The little girl tugged my sleeve again, and I jerked away, imagining her fingers brushing across the scar tissue on my wrists, imagining that the red material of the Santa suit was stained with my blood.

"Please let me tell you my wish."

"Okay." I pushed away my memories, feeling a strange combination of sorrow and glee. "But you have to tell me something first. Have you been a good girl this year?"

Her forehead wrinkled in deep thought—and my heart melted a little more because I'd forgotten all the perfectly genuine expressions that kids have—and then she gave me a very serious nod. "I think so. Mommy says that I'm a good girl all the time."

"I'm sure your mom wouldn't lie," I said. "Now, you give me the word, and I'll give it to the big guy at the North Pole."

She moved closer, and her voice became a whisper. "I don't want any toys." She paused and looked around, as if someone might be listening to her little secret, as if an eavesdropper could render the wish null and void in Santa's eyes. "I just want Santa to bring me a brand new daddy for Christmas. And I want him to make my real daddy go away."

My heart skittered, then started beating faster. I looked at the little girl and suddenly saw my daughter, and a hot sheen of sweat dampened my face.

You're not my daddy.

My mouth was running before I knew what to say. "Now, sweetie, I'm not so sure that Santa Claus can bring you that type of present. Wouldn't you rather have a pretty new dress?" *Or a coat that fits?* I thought, looking again at the tattered thing she was wearing.

She didn't say anything, but that didn't keep me from hearing the other voice in my head. *You're not my daddy, because you're a bad man.*

And then I was apologizing, alibiing for a man I didn't even know. "Look," I continued. "I'll bet your dad will get you something nice. I'll bet he already has a great big present for you right under the tree. I'll bet—"

"No!" A tear rolled down her cheek, and she wiped it away before anyone else could see it. "I don't *like* my daddy's presents. I want a new daddy, someone to make me and mommy happy. I just have to get one. You gotta help me."

Suddenly the Santa costume felt as heavy as a suit of armor, all the weight centered on my chest and stomach. And for the first time since going straight three years before, I thought of just how lucky my little girl was to have a real father now, someone to watch over her and protect her and love her. Someone who wasn't a *bad man* ... even if he was a damn chiropractor.

My eyes misted over and I closed them. I didn't know what to say. I sent my own wish to Santa, Fed Ex. All I wanted for Christmas was the right answer for this little girl.

"Julie, what in the world have you done to Santa?"

I opened my eyes. The girl's mother was younger than I would have guessed, late twenties probably. A mirror image of her daughter, another waif in faded jeans and a worn jacket, carrying a single Parker's shopping bag.

I grinned. This time it was a reflex. I really didn't know what to do.

"I sure hope Julie hasn't been bothering you," the woman said. "I got held up in line and—" The woman smiled and tousled Julie's hair. She was every bit as beautiful as her daughter, and every bit as tragic. Her eyes held the same sadness, but they never flashed bright the way her child's sometimes did. They were the eyes of a woman who had faced too much pain in her time and had given up the fight. Someone who was merely existing, not living.

Someone just like me.

"Well, I'll apologize anyway," the woman said. "Julie's a good girl"—Julie nudged my leg, as if to say *I told you so*—" but she can be a bit headstrong." The woman made a polite show of checking her watch. "Julie, honey, we really have to get going. We're already an hour late. You know how your father gets when his dinner isn't waiting for him."

"Okay. In a minute, Mom."

I smiled at the friendly mother-daughter battle waging before me, recalling the occasions when my wife and daughter had done the same.

But those days were gone.

You're not my daddy....

"Well, thanks again for being so nice to Julie," the woman said. "And have a Merry Christmas." She took Julie's hand. "Let's go, honey."

They were swallowed by the crowd and, just like that, the incident was over. Or so I thought.

A few seconds later, the little angel reappeared. "I almost forgot," she said, panting. "Please tell Santa this is where I live."

She handed me a piece of paper. The lined kind you tear from a small tablet. Three short sentences in careful block print. A street address that wasn't far from the mall.

Her hand drifted away slowly. Brushed my big black belt. Brushed the front of my red pants.

Her fingers lingered for just a second against my crotch.

She looked at me with those lonely eyes. "I'll do anything," she said. "Tell Santa I'll do anything if he gives me what I want."

Then her hand was gone, and she was gone, and everything was very clear.

I just want Santa to bring me a brand new daddy for Christmas. And then I want him to make my real daddy go away....

You know how your father gets when his dinner isn't waiting for him....

I don't like my daddy's presents....

I'll do anything ... tell Santa I'll do anything if he gives me what I want....

I stared at the slip of paper with Julie's address on it, thinking about the fierce determination on the little angel's face and the sad quiet beauty of her mother, knowing with complete clarity how life had molded them.

Understanding, for the first time, how life had molded me.

§

I called in sick more than I should have, made use of my days off, didn't sleep much. You can always find time to do things if you really want to, and I found that I wanted to do something for the first time in years. Besides, it wasn't like I had a ton of unfinished Christmas shopping or invitations demanding my presence at holiday parties hither and yon. No airplane ride to visit the relatives out west. No drive in the country to visit friends. No Christmas in Connecticut for me.

No, my social schedule was clear. I spent my time with Julie and her family, though they never knew that I was around.

The rusted mailbox in front of the house said *COOPER*. The house itself looked like any other in the neighborhood, just another old ranch-style thing that needed work—new gutters, energy-efficient windows, some paint. There were no Christmas lights hanging from the eaves, no tree in the window. That wasn't unusual—more than a few of the Cooper's neighbors seemed to be getting along without the prescribed signs of seasonal cheer. The neighborhood was definitely not upwardly mobile, more like we're-holding-on-by-the-skin-of-our-teeth. But Julie's was the only house on the block where the snow mounded unshoveled on the walk, the only house where a television antenna stood in for a cable hookup.

None of that really surprised me, not at first. I'd seen the way Julie and Tina—that was her mom's name—dressed. I'd followed them to enough discount markets and cheap gas stations to know that things were tight with them.

I wasn't really surprised until I saw Julie's father for the first time. He glided past my parked car late one evening, lounging behind the wheel of a black Cadillac Seville that shone like a new eight-ball. He parked next to the rattletrap Datsun that Tina drove, a hunk of Japanese metal that looked like Godzilla had had his way with it.

A couple days passed before our schedules meshed. Then I followed Mr. Cooper instead of Julie and Tina.

I hated him instantly. For one thing, he worked for the phone company. He was a big enough fish to warrant his own parking space, and he made a habit of taking the bigger fish to lunch and picking up the tab. I followed him into places where I could barely afford the price of a Diet Coke and a bowl of soup. I watched as he left generous tips for the waiters, and I don't think I'll ever forget the satisfied little smirk that crossed his lips when he gave his boss a pen-and-pencil set from Parker's, a shoplifter's favorite that would have set me back several day's pay. After work, Cooper stopped off for drinks at a bar near the highway, a dive called the High Hat Club. Dropped more tip money, though he kept to himself. Didn't spare the booze, either. He was always pretty well tanked by the time he headed home.

All this while his wife and daughter lived like paupers.

That wasn't the only reason I disliked Julie's dad, though.

His first name was Adrian. That went right along with the little smirk.

And Adrian Cooper liked to rape his daughter.

It happened on weekends as far as I could tell. Tina actually had a job on Saturday and Sunday at a run-down florist shop over by the mall, but I knew the job was just a ploy to get her out of the house.

I sat in my car on two consecutive weekends, trying not to be noticed on that gray little street. Four days, and every one of them was the same. Tina would leave for work. Shortly thereafter, the drapes would whisper closed, and the lights would be extinguished. The last drape to close and the last light to dim were always in Julie's bedroom.

Several hours passed each time. Then the lights came on and the drapes were opened, after which Adrian packed the sullen little girl with the porcelain complexion into his big black car and treated her to an ice-cream sundae at the mall. I'm sure that in his sick little mind that trip to the mall made everything okay with him. The son of a bitch couldn't even see it. Slurping up his ice cream, fingers drumming so innocently on his pale daughter's knee.

Four days of that, and I saw everything as if I had x-ray vision. I sat there in my old car, watching the minutes tick by on the dashboard clock. It was all I could do to stay behind the wheel while it happened.

And then the last Sunday came, the Sunday before Christmas, and suddenly I realized I was done sitting.

The Caddy pulled out and headed for the mall. I made a U-turn and parked in front of the rusted mailbox that said *COOPER*. I got out and walked up the drive, and I didn't even bother to knock because no one who lived on the gray little street was paying attention.

I kicked in the door. Like I said, there wasn't a Christmas tree, but there were a few presents. It didn't surprise me that most of them were addressed to "Adrian" or "Daddy." I collected a stack, took them out to the car, and dumped them in the backseat, just to make it look good. I waited to hear the sirens, but there was no sound at all.

I returned to the house, and this time I closed the door behind me. Adrian and Tina had separate bedrooms. Adrian, of course, occupied the largest in the house.

It was a fairly boring room. Dull—if tasteful—furniture, stupid little Sharper Image gadgets, uninspiring prints on the wall, and a bed with a very hard mattress.

A stout, masculine dresser stood to the right of the bed. I searched the drawers and found stiff pin-striped shirts and argyle socks and other clothes that seemed designed especially for a phone company fast-track kind of guy. Other drawers housed Ralph Lauren clothes for fast-track-kind-of-guy weekends.

In the bottom drawer, beneath Adrian's Polo sweaters, I found a pistol.

So, the bastard was smart enough to be a little paranoid.

I figured the pistol was a sign that I was getting close. I pulled up the lining paper glued to the bottom of the drawer. A large envelope was hidden underneath, along with a few kiddie porn magazines.

I dumped the pictures on the hard bed and saw the little girl with the face of an angel doing the things her daddy made her do.

But I only looked at her eyes.

§

After I left the house, I drove over to the florist shop and parked next to the battle-scarred Datsun with four balding tires.

Tina was inside, busily misting some ferns that hung near the cash register. I thought that she looked good in the cheap pink blouse with her name stitched over the pocket, and then our eyes met, and I found myself remembering Julie's eyes in Cooper's secret pictures.

"Can I help you?" she asked, and it sounded like she'd break apart if I refused the offer.

"I hope you can." I tried to make it light, but I was a bundle of nerves. "I guess I'm just not a white Christmas kind of guy. I want something green. You know, something nice. Not a fern or anything. Something with flowers."

Her eyes narrowed. "I don't mean to sound weird or anything," she said. "But your voice—it sounds really familiar. Have we met?"

"Picture me with a long white beard."

"What?"

"Santa Claus." I smiled and found the expression was becoming a little more comfortable. "Parker's Department Store version, at your service."

She laughed, and it was a good sound. "I thought we'd met."

"Yeah. I guess there's something about a man in red that

makes a lasting impression."

We stood there for a moment, staring at each other, and then she went into florist-shop mode. "So," she said, looking around, "we've established that you're not a fern kind of guy. Is this for a gift?"

"No. It's for me. I just want a little something to, y'know, brighten things up."

"If you want bright, maybe you should get another string of lights for your tree."

I shrugged. "I don't have a tree. I live alone." The statement sounded too blunt, so I tried to lighten it. "It's a real small apartment. I need all the oxygen for myself."

That fell flat.

"Sorry," Tina said. The word slipped out as a sigh, and she left it at that. I recognized the ploy. She didn't *ask* any questions because she didn't want to be *asked* any questions.

"So?" I said.

"How about this?" She was smiling now, holding a little pot with some kind of miniature bush in it.

"I don't know," I said. "I'm looking for something with flowers. And this looks like one of those Japanese bonsai things—"

"No." Her voice brightened. "It blooms. It's a miniature rose."

"What color?"

"White."

I nodded, and we moved over to the cash register. The top button of her blouse was undone, and I could still see the porcelain skin of her neck ... and the bruise that began at her collarbone and ran God knows where.

She cringed a little, raising her arm, working the register buttons. I didn't say anything, even though the picture of her husband's little smirk was locked up tight in my head without possibility of parole. *Fair trade*, that smirk said, *a little pain for a late dinner.*

She took my money, and I started for the door. Then something inside me switched gears, and I stopped short. "I've got a question for you," I said.

"Shoot."

"Miniature roses—if you treat them right, do they grow up to be regular roses?"

She shrugged. "I really don't know."

I stood there a moment, just to let a beat pass, and then I shrugged. "Well, I guess I'll just have to wait and find out for myself."

"You'll let me know?" Tina asked.

"I'll let you know," I said.

I didn't realize then, but it was the first promise I'd made in years.

§

The black Caddy with the billiard ball shine pulled away from the parking spot marked *A. COOPER*, and I followed it into the night.

Adrian had worked late—three hours overtime by my estimation—but that didn't matter to me. Now that his day was over, everything was going to go smoothly. Adrian was going to hit the High Hat Club. I was going to join him. Belly up with Mr. Fast Track and strike up a conversation. If that was possible. Order a beer, my first in three years, and hold myself to just one, if *that* was possible (and I prayed that it was). Maybe we'd talk about the kind of magazines that came in brown paper wrappers, or trade tips about how to find camera shops that were willing to print pictures of naked children if you were willing to shell out some of the cash your wife and kid never saw. In short, I wanted to watch old Adrian sweat a little bit, just so I would know what that looked like. I wanted to see him loosen his expensive tie, and I wanted to sniff the air and learn just how effective his expensive deodorant was.

But if he was all chatted out after a tough day shilling 800 numbers, that was okay too. I could wait. I could bide my time. Either way, when Adrian left the High Hat, I planned to be right behind him, closer than he could imagine. Closer even than his own shadow.

The Caddy eased onto the freeway and dipped into traffic. I followed. I was signaling for the exit near the High Hat when Adrian changed lanes and headed south. Sweat beaded on my forehead, and a hole seemed to open up in my guts. This wasn't right. This wasn't supposed to happen.

And then Adrian's turn signal was flashing. He took the Briarwood exit, traveled a road I knew by heart, and made the same turn I'd made morning after morning for the last three years, ever since I'd gotten sober.

There weren't many empty parking spaces, it being the Monday before Christmas, so Adrian Cooper parked his Caddy in a handicapped spot near the big glass doors of the mall that housed Parker's Department Store.

§

I started to worry when closing time came and there was no sign of Mr. Adrian Cooper. Then I remembered what kind of guy he was. Cooper certainly thought he held a paramount spot in the universe. Such an important personage wouldn't think anything of holding up a few working stiffs so he could get what he wanted.

The thought got under my skin and stayed there. As if on cue, Adrian exited the mall's smoked glass doors. A slash of bright light knifed across my feet, and then the door whispered closed and the light was gone. I stood to one side of the door, just some nobody Adrian had to step around, and I welcomed the shadows and the soft green light that painted the snow-covered parking lot.

Adrian's expensive loafers crunched over the fresh snow. He balanced a stack of boxes which were wrapped in the signature silver-foil wrap of my employer.

The Caddy was one of two cars parked in the first row.

Adrian noticed what I'd left for him quicker than I'd expected.

"Shit," he muttered, setting the boxes on the hood of the Caddy and snatching something from under the windshield wiper.

It wasn't what he had expected. It wasn't a parking ticket.

His knees actually quivered. He nearly went down. I enjoyed seeing that.

I walked over and took the little picture of Julie out of his hand.

"This is what it feels like," I said.

He didn't seem to hear me. I took the keys out of his hands, opened the door before he could protest.

"We have to talk," I said, lowering a leather-gloved hand on his shoulder, pushing him into the car.

§

The first thing Adrian did was loosen his tie. Then he started to sweat, and the Caddy was choked with a scent both raw and spicy.

We were parked at the edge of the mall lot, next to a chain-link fence that rimmed a Christmas tree lot. The hour was late and the lot was closed. All I could see was a sprinkling of dim white Christmas lights; a giant inflatable Santa, arms bobbing under the weight of fresh snowflakes; and the stark, spindly silhouettes of the cheap, dead trees.

"I bet Julie would like a tree," I said.

Adrian Cooper nodded.

I laughed, kicked at the silver paper around my feet, and shifted the boxes so my hands were free. "You know, she still believes in Santa Claus."

Adrian sputtered, "I—I didn't realize that."

"And you know what else?" He didn't reply, but our eyes met, and it killed me that even in this moment his blue eyes held more spark than either Tina's or Julie's. "No," I continued, "you don't know, so I'll tell you. Julie knows something most seven-year-olds don't know. She knows how to come on to Santa Claus. She's a little kid who had to learn how to whore just to survive. And you taught her that. You're the one who twisted her."

Cooper's hands were tight on the steering wheel. He didn't say a word.

"Aren't you going to offer me money?" I asked.

"I ... I don't think ... you want money."

"You're right about that." I reached into my coat, and my fingers closed around the pistol I'd taken from Adrian's stout, masculine dresser. "You know, I had a wife and kid once. A little girl, just like Julie. A woman just as pretty as Tina. I blew it with them. Oh, not as bad as you. Not nearly as bad as you. But I blew it. See, I was a smash-up-the-family-car kind of guy, a come-get-me-out-of-jail kind of husband. A sorry-I-missed-Christmas kind of dad.

"With me it was the bottle. That's a sickness. But I woke up and saw it. I faced it down until I memorized every ugly scale on the monster's hide. And I learned how to control it. Things are better now."

Adrian's voice was very quiet. "Maybe I can ..." He hesitated, searching for the right word.

I found it for him. "Change? Maybe you can. I'm not saying it's impossible. But I don't think that it's going to happen. And I don't think Julie and Tina can count on the odds you'd give them."

One hand stayed on the pistol. The other hand drifted over one of the boxes from Parker's Department Store. My gloved fingers brushed the wisps of red silk nestled in tissue paper. I hooked the spaghetti straps, lifted the teddy, and watched it dance in the shadows. It didn't seem any bigger than a handkerchief, really.

"Amazing," I said. "I didn't know that they made these things so small. What did you tell the salesgirl, anyway? You tell her that your wife was Vietnamese?"

"Look," Adrian said, "if you're going to do something—"

I slipped the gun from my pocket. I could hardly feel it with my hands sheathed in heavy gloves.

"Wait a minute." His blue eyes were focused on me instead of the gun. "I know this is going to happen. I know I can't stop you. But I think it would be easier on both of us if you give me the gun. I'd rather do this myself."

I thought it over. I really wanted to believe him.

But I couldn't, and that was sad. "I can't play those odds, Cooper," I said.

He closed his eyes. I stared down at the Christmas card, which had been covered by the skimpy teddy. On the front, a cartoon man wearing a goofy grin, saying, "You're invited to trim my tree." On the inside flap, same man, naked and grotesque. "All it takes is two red balls."

Under that, scrawled in expensive ink from a Parker's Department Store pen:

Love My Little Girl,

Daddy

Adrian Cooper said, "Are you sure—"
He never finished the sentence.

§

When they lowered the coffin into the grave, I was thinking that it should have been wrapped with a big red bow.

Tina and Julie buried Adrian Cooper on Christmas morning. I interpreted that as a good sign, a sign that Tina wanted to lay the past to rest and move on. No one else attended the funeral but the minister, and he was in and out in a matter of minutes. Everyone's busy on Christmas.

Everyone but me.

I stayed in the shadows, standing over the grave of a man I didn't know with flowers in my hands. It looked like Adrian's death would be ruled a suicide. I had been pretty careful—I'd worn gloves when I pulled the trigger, and then, after Adrian was dead, I'd twisted his fingers around the weapon and fired a shot through the open window. And if there wasn't a suicide note, the ripped up greeting card, torn photos, and lingerie seemed to stand in pretty well in the minds of the homicide detectives.

Still, I wasn't willing to take any unnecessary chances by getting too close to the ceremony. Cops love to watch funerals, I'm told. So I viewed the proceedings from a distance, and I saw a little girl and her mother standing over a dirt grave rimmed by a meadow of snow, their faces showing nothing, but their fingers interlocked.

I guessed it was as good a start as any. God knows there have been worse. But the real start came a moment later, when the two of them turned and walked toward Tina's Datsun.

I had to stop myself from chasing after them, and it was probably the hardest thing I've ever done. I stood there in the cold, flowers gripped in my gloved hands, remembering the deuce of hearts I'd drawn on the day I met Julie. I thought of her father and his black heart, and I wondered what color my heart was after all I'd done.

The Datsun took off under a cloud of smoke. Four bald tires

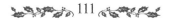 111

left black lines in the snow.

And everything was very quiet.

Snow dusted the gravestones, so very white. I thought about the white rose sitting all alone in my apartment, and the gray little neighborhood where Tina and Julie lived. All those houses that no one seemed to care about. Maybe one of them was waiting for someone to come along and give it some special attention.

I found, to my surprise, that I was making plans again, but this time they were the kind of plans that were meant to be shared.

And standing there in the snow, I began to wonder how soon my miniature rose would flower.

FROM A CHRISTMAS PAST
(STORIES FROM CHRISTMAS HORROR VOLUME 2)

A NOTE FROM SANTA

William F. Nolan

o you believe in ghosts? Well, *I* sure do. With good reason. I *met* one, a real nasty one. I'd just gone down the chimney of this home in Kansas City. Old part of town. Rundown. But I had to stop off and deliver some toys to this little ten-year-old brat, which I did. Left 'em by the big Christmas tree in the living room. The kid was still asleep.

And that's when this ghost showed up, fierce-looking. A mean SOB, that's for sure. Lemme tell you, not all ghosts are vapory. This one was solid. Came at me with an axe!

Swung it at me. I ducked under the blade and lit out for the chimney. Climbed back to the roof. Looked down. There he was, peering up the chimney at me and shaking his axe.

Well, as I was watching him, he just began misting away, till there was nothing left of him but his axe. Oh, he was a ghost all right. No doubt of that.

I was lucky to be alive!

And that's why I believe in ghosts.

LITTLE WARRIORS

Gene O'Neill

Prologue

On Mt. George, near the Monticello-to-Napa old wagon trail, December 2015—

Around midnight, near the still standing redwood shed, which had served in the past as a halfway horse-changing station for the wagons back-hauling quicksilver to Napa from Monticello, hundreds of greenish-blue dots coalesced into a luminescent existence. For a moment, the amorphous figure, about the size of a large hummingbird, hovered as if gaining its bearings; then, just an iridescent blur, it zoomed three quarters of the way up Mt. George and quickly disappeared beneath the shadowed decking extending across the western face of the darkened adobe home.

1.

The Arthur Brothers, Jake and Little Anthony—his nickname ironic because he stood six-foot-three, only half an inch shorter than his older brother—were waiting for their sidekick, Wilton Smith Jr. Wilton, better known on the Oakland streets as Repeat, was shopping to find a properly fitting set of snowshoes for his childlike feet. The recently paroled trio had already been to two

117

other places, including REI in Berkeley, with no luck, and the brothers were now waiting impatiently outside Snowdrift Ski Shop in Moraga, standing next to their '91 Escort station wagon—a heavily decorated survivor of the Oakland parking wars.

The ex-cons had made recent plans for a series of potential big-score burglaries, but they'd all need snowshoes for the robberies. They planned on taking advantage of the early snow flurries right after Thanksgiving and the subsequent heavier snowfalls in December that had recently closed down State Highway 89 around the southwestern edge of Lake Tahoe.

"Lots of wealthy hot shots from the Bay Area have cabins isolated by the snow up there now," Little Anthony had explained earlier in the day—he was the leader of the group. "We'll borrow Big Mack's four-wheel-drive Dodge Ram pickup, break in to a couple of the boarded-up smaller cabins just off 89 at night; and then the next day we'll hit some of the bigger chalets nearer Squaw Valley and the other ski lifts. If the rich people are even up there for Christmas vacation, you can bet your sweet asses they'll be off skiing during the day, leaving behind all their expensive Christmas presents still wrapped."

The smaller man appeared suddenly, running out of the front doors of Snowdrift, quickly approaching the parked junker and proudly waving his new pair of children's snowshoes overhead like two tennis rackets, grinning excitedly, but stalling out when he tried to explain: "L-L-L-L—"

Jake put his arm around his hyper cohort's shoulders, hugged him tightly, and quietly said: "Okay, Bro. Now ya just take a deep breath in and out ... and calm the fook down, ya unnerstan what I'm sayin."

Repeat nodded, sucked in a long breath, let it out slowly, and then tried to talk again, but could only manage: "G-G-G—" He stomped his foot violently on the asphalt, which jarred loose an explosive: "Got em, fellas!"

To a casual stranger, his stunted stature, pronounced stammer and bizarre facial tics made Repeat appear physically/intellectually challenged. But even though the little ex-con was gullible, naïve, and childlike at times, he was also a certified badass in a tight spot. He'd once saved Little Anthony from being slashed on the main yard at San Quentin by charging and head-butting a Black Guerilla, knocking the prison gang member flat on his back, and then disarming the semi-conscious man of his weapon—a piece of safety razor melted into the head of a plastic toothbrush handle. Fortunately for them, all three friends were transferred to the CCC near Susanville, a minimum-security prison camp in Northern California, a few days after the hushed-up incident without having to face Department of Corrections discipline or, more importantly, deadly BG retaliation. The Arthur Brothers never forgot Repeat's brave action.

2.

Tanner McKinney waited anxiously at the foot of the Southwest Airline Terminal escalator to the baggage claim on the street level at Oakland Airport for Sally and the twins to appear. Their flight from San Diego had been delayed over an hour and a half by regional thunderstorms, which seldom, if ever, occurred in San Diego in December. He was anxious because Sally and the kids had been living with her older sister, Lilly, in Carlsbad during a trial separation. He hadn't seen any of them for over three months. Now, he was hopeful that the family could finally be reunited permanently. He was going to do his best to make it happen, and it sounded like Sally was more than a bit willing to give it a sincere try. She'd agreed on spending the kids' *entire* Christmas vacation at his family's adobe cabin isolated on the western slope of Mt. George—the highest point on the eastern side of Napa Valley. He was relieved because his earliest memories as a youngster included the yearly McKinney Clan tradition of gathering for Christmas at the adobe on Mt. George. In recent years, the extended family had been shrinking in numbers, due to some of the younger members having moved away from the Bay Area, but also an increasing number older family members passing. Now, it was just Tanner, his immediate family, and his brother, Mike. He was thankful they would be reunited and continue the thirty-plus years of McKinney Christmas tradition atop Mt. George.

Tanner was busy scanning the faces of descending passengers, afraid he'd miss his family in the tightly-packed departure crowd. Sally was petite, the twins mirroring her tiny stature. As his family appeared in view, so did his favorite Christmas carol, "The Little Drummer Boy," throughout the terminal—*Brrrum, brum, brum, brum ...*

"Hey, Pops," Sean shouted, waving as he led the family onto the down escalator. The fourteen-year-old wasn't usually so publicly demonstrative. But Sinead, his twin sister, was right behind him, characteristically jumping up and down, waving over peoples' heads. Sally brought up the rear, looking down at him and smiling broadly.

Because of the long hours at his computer day job at Cisco Systems and then writing half the night and every weekend during the year past, Sally had complained of him being inattentive to the family. It was true, he had not been there for any of them. But he'd really ignored all three during the last six months, because he thought he was on the verge of breaking into the big time with one of his thriller novels. He'd secured a good NYC agent who had agreed with that assessment of *The New Plague,* but had forwarded along thirty or so single-spaced pages of suggested complicated edits and revisions. Then, in the middle of those revisions at the end of last August, Sally had shocked him, taking matters into her own hands, abruptly packing up some necessities, and leaving their apartment in San Francisco with the kids for Carlsbad.

Negotiations over the phone the last week or so had been promising. Watching them descend on the escalator, Tanner waved back, his spirit lifting and taking the edge off his nervousness.

On the ground floor, they all hugged, Sally kissing him on the lips—just a trace firmer than an old-garden-variety-greeting peck. And she whispered: "Missed you, Mr. T." So, the family huddled up and chatted about the flight delay, while they waited five minutes to pick up their luggage. Then, bags in hand, Tanner led them to the parked Lexus SUV with the tiny Christmas tree riding in the rack on top. As was traditional, the family would decorate a tree at the adobe.

Even at 4 o'clock, the Friday night commuter traffic from the

Oakland Airport west on I-880 and then north on I-80 was gridlocked, much worse than usual. With school out for Christmas vacation, perhaps many were already heading up to the ski resorts at Stateline and Lake Tahoe—there had been a flurry of snowstorms right after Thanksgiving up until the present. The stop-and-go progress on the freeway gave the family a chance to relax, everyone perhaps feeling a bit stiff after the almost four-month separation. The constant stream of Christmas music on the radio also helped put everyone in a relaxed, joyful mood.

Tanner asked the kids about their new school. The twins had been good students in San Francisco, and were presently enrolled in the eighth-grade at the famed Children's School near UC San Diego in LaJolla.

"Going great, Pops," Sean said. "Our modern Christmas play was really fun and turned out well. Good audience reactions. I helped write it and was a kinda hippie guru wearing a tie-dyed outfit. Sinead starred as San Diego Lou, a country-western guitar player, who sang, "Crazy" and "Mamas Don't Let Your Babies Grow Up To Be—"

"Sean, you were supposed to let *me* tell Dad!" Sinead interrupted.

Her brother shrugged and said, "Oh, *sorry*," his dismissive tone indicating he wasn't the least bit concerned about his sister's disappointed outburst.

Both rambled on about the new school, their teachers, and especially a bunch of new friends. Sounded to Tanner like they both had adjusted exceptionally well for teenagers being disrupted from their routine on short notice, and then leaving behind all their old friends at University Middle School in San Francisco.

"Dad, did Uncle Mike get off work early in Sacramento, and will he be here tonight at the cabin?" Sinead asked. The twins were tight with his much younger, single brother. Mike had bonded with them when they were ten-years-old, teaching them basic and advanced archery skills and taking them to many junior competitions around the country. Recently, he'd told Tanner and Sally that he thought the twins had the ability to compete internationally, perhaps even a chance of making the Olympic archery team and going to Rio de Janeiro next year, but probably a lock for making the team for Tokyo in 2020.

Tanner smiled inwardly. His brother was a lifelong skilled bow hunter, and had promised to take the twins deer and boar hunting when they turned sixteen. A year ago, Mike had set up a tough training schedule, the pair practicing religiously three days a week at the South City Archer's Club; then, on weekends whenever possible, they would go up and shoot at least one day at Mike's private archery club near Rocklin—Billy Tell's Red Apple Range.

"Not tonight, but Uncle Mike will be up late tomorrow evening or early Sunday morning," Tanner said.

"He's planning on staying on for Christmas Eve, right?" Sally asked.

Tanner nodded. "He said he wouldn't miss it, had some special gifts for his *favorite* niece and nephew."

"We're his *only* niece and nephew, Pops," Sean said, chuckling at his uncle's old joke.

The family was fairly relaxed now, enjoying each other's company and the background Christmas music, even though the commuter traffic was still stop-and-go.... But eventually it thinned significantly as they crossed over the Carquinez Bridge on I-80 and passed by the eastern turn-off for Benicia on the southern outskirts of Vallejo.

"Looks like it'll be too dark to practice anyhow if we *ever* do get to the cabin this evening," Sinead complained, disappointed resignation obvious in her tone. It was already beginning to turn dusk. They'd both been working on their quick pull, aim, and release technique at pop-ups at a San Diego archery club, but they wanted to get down as soon as possible to practice the technique at the new target range their uncle had cleared: a long level spot near the old Monticello-to-Napa historic wagon trail—a pair of stationary targets using the horse shed as a backdrop.

"You guys can go down tomorrow morning, get in some practice before Uncle Mike gets here," Sally suggested. She'd strongly encouraged the small but athletic youngsters' almost obsessive interest in archery, although she was alarmed by Mike's recent offer to take them out bow hunting a year or so from now. That sounded a bit too dangerous to her.

Tanner glanced at the twins in the back seat, smiled, and nodded. "You can show off for Uncle Mike tomorrow night or Sunday morning after he gets here."

At about 7:10, the McKinney family finally pulled into the circular driveway in front of the family place. Then they hauled their luggage into the sprawling adobe. Quickly dropping off their stuff into the three bedrooms, they all met out on the long deck spanning the back of the house and enjoyed the spectacular view, everywhere below them Napa Christmas lights sparkling. After a few minutes, Tanner walked to the southern end of the deck, looked down, and checked out the attached old-fashioned greenhouse. Everything was still apparently intact, including all the multi-paned glass windows. Overhead, the stars were twinkling, and to the south, thirty-five miles away, the red and green lights from San Francisco were shining brightly, as were the lights of St. Helena, away up-valley about ten or eleven miles. As the family enjoyed the sights, the full moon rose over the mountain behind them, bathing the Napa Valley directly below them in silvery, eerie moonlight.

Sinead stared down at the barely visible old wagon trail looping around from northeast to southwest halfway down the mountain, and then said: "Look, you can even make out the two archery targets Uncle Mike set up behind the horse-changing shed."

Tanner nodded and said: "Some of your great-grandfather Harry's ashes are scattered beside that horse shed ... just north of that nearby spring." The spring had been capped long ago, and a deep depression left unfilled was hidden by ground cover, including wild blackberries, growing thickly.

"Your gramps personally built that redwood horse shed, right, Pops?" Sean said.

"Yes, just after he built this adobe and great viewing porch...." Thinking back for a moment, Tanner laughed. "When I first came up here as a youngster, the old boy had five hummingbird feeders hanging along this decking. He loved and admired the feisty little devils as his *personal* animal totems. Claimed they showed some of our family's Gaelic fighting spirit. In fact, he often called them: 'Little Warriors.'" Tanner smiled wryly to himself. Even folks who knew Gramps well would've never guessed the tough old bird's private hobby back then. He'd built the greenhouse attached to the south side of the house to raise rare orchids.

"Harry was indeed an interesting man," Sally said, leading the others back inside the sliding glass doors. She'd never met the family patriarch, who'd died thirty-some years ago, but she'd heard many of the McKinney family legends about his nature and exploits. "After finally retiring at seventy-seven he'd hiked for a month above 15,000 feet in the Himalayas."

Later that night, they decorated the Christmas tree, brought in and spread out the presents from the car. They'd actually begin their yearly tradition tomorrow night reading a Christmas story, and opening one present each of the five nights before Christmas Eve. Saturday night, it would be Sinead's turn to read O. Henry's wonderful Christmas story, "The Gift of the Magi."

Early Saturday morning Sinead rushed into her mom and dad's master bedroom, her cheeks a rosy red and shouted: "Come quick, outside! You guys aren't going to believe this."

Alarmed, the parents struggled up out of the warm tangle of covers, hurrying into a *freezing* front room in their skimpy night clothes—the twin had left the front door wide open.

Everywhere outside was totally blanketed in white, including where Sean was standing in the middle of the circular driveway near the storage shed.

It had snowed last night while they all were sleeping.

The adults looked around with disbelief, because it *never* snowed here in the Valley ... or anywhere in the Bay Area. But it had last night, and it'd been heavy. The snow was deep enough to almost cover Sean's Converses—

Barefoot, Sally shivered in her thin negligee, and with teeth chattering she said to the family: "Let's all get back inside before we freeze and dress up warmer. Maybe get a cup of hot chocolate down, before we come back out to play in this strange stuff." Of course they didn't have gloves or snow parkas or even hooded winter coats, but they could all wear sweatshirts under their lined raincoats. Sally had fortunately packed them for her and the twins, and had insisted that Tanner bring his along in case. There was occasionally *some* rain in the valley in December, and especially up here on Mt. George.

3.

Naturally, Jake, Little Anthony, and Repeat had adjusted their plans, as soon as they saw it snowing earlier that morning and heard the Bay Area weather forecasts—a fifty-year snowstorm was predicted to hit later, a possible whiteout at higher elevations by nightfall. They realized they didn't have to drive five or six hours from Oakland up to Tahoe for good isolated burglary targets. Instead, Little Anthony had suggested: "Let's head up to the Napa Valley, lots of rich people with places in the eastern foothills. Me and Jake know that area pretty well."

Repeat grinned and said: "G-G-Good deal."

"Yeah, years ago, when we were jus kids livin in nearby American Canyon, we caddied at the swanky Napa Country Club off Hagen Road," Jake said. "Ha, before they fired our raggedy asses, ya unnerstan."

"W-what for?" Repeat asked.

"The caddy master claimed we were stealin cigarettes, lighters, gum, and change from customers' golf bags," Jake replied and shrugged with a sly grin. "So we kicked the shit out of him, and then gotta hat. We knew the pussy would sic the cops on us if we hung around."

He ended the story right there ... and the three cohorts all laughed with devilish delight.

4.

It began snowing again before noon, and by mid-afternoon in some places it was almost a foot deep, especially along the south side of the adobe and greenhouse, smaller drifts piling up on the exposed hundred yards or so of the narrow access road before it wound down northeasterly and disappeared into the cover of the thick forest of madrone, oak, and pine trees.

Mike had called just before dinner, and said that he'd heard about the freak snowstorm in the Valley, but he still planned on being up there sometime tomorrow morning. He drove an older Jeep for hunting, which had four-wheel drive and good tires. State Highway 121 up from the Napa Valley floor would probably be plowed clear by then, he'd said, because it was the only access from Napa to Wooden Valley and the town of Winters. And the mile of unplowed private steep road that turned off 121 and climbed up the leeward side of the mountain to the adobe was fairly well protected by the thick forest. So, Uncle Mike was confident of making it despite the predicted heavy snowfall later in the evening.

5.

By dark, the three ex-cons had driven to the eastern Napa Valley foothills, the end of Hagen Road, which actually merged with the non-graded southern end of the historic Monticello-to-Napa wagon trail. In the four-wheel drive pickup they made it as far as possible along the narrow, rocky trail, parking close to the less steep southern slope of Mt. George. First they put on their disguises as the three Wise Men—striped bathrobes and towels wrapped on their heads as turbans. If they got stopped by the law on the way up or leaving, they'd claim they were going to a Christmas party. Then they slipped into their snowshoes and backpacks. Repeat was armed with a sawed-off ten-gauge shotgun, and the Arthur brothers both carried Glock 9mm automatics, K-bars, and plastic handcuffs in their backpacks. They began plodding the quarter of a mile along the old wagon trail, then climbed straight up a draw toward lights shining in a place about three-quarters of the way up the mountain. Had to be rich guys living way up there....

They finally stopped to catch their breath at the steps leading up to a long porch, took their nylon stocking masks out of their backpacks, and slipped them on.

6.

After wolfing down a microwave pizza, the family was gathered around the big dining room table to listen to Sinead read "The Gift of the Magi." She'd neared the end of the ironic story, where the poor, young couple are exchanging their wrapped presents. He'd sold his only valuable possession, an antique watch, to buy her a decorated comb for her beautiful hair; and she'd sold her long tresses to buy him a watch fob.

At that moment Sally glanced up ... and sucked in a gasp. Three 2,000 year-old revenants resembling the Wise Men, supernaturally conjured up by the story were hovering and looking in the porch window. She finally managed a scream.

The oddly dressed figures, with weirdly distorted features, were sliding the unlocked glass door fully open.

"Hey, hold it, right there!" Tanner shouted, jumping up from the table, hurrying across the dining room, and confronting the intruders, who were all wearing nylon stocking masks disguising their faces.

"S-S-Shut up," the smallest man said, stepping forward and deftly tapping Tanner squarely in the face with the butt of his shotgun.

Tanner retained consciousness, but sagged to his knees, cupping his hand to his bloody nose and cut lip. By then the family was upset and badly frightened.

Sally overcame her initial shock, moved over and kneeled at Tanner's side, trying to staunch the bleeding with her apron.

"Okay, folks," one of the big men said calmly, but gesturing with an automatic handgun, "no one needs to get hurt like Sir Galahad here, *if* y'all listen carefully and follow orders. Okay?"

The stunned twins remained seated, but speechless and looking wide-eyed at the armed spokesman ...but finally nodded.

"Anyone armed, or guns stashed here?"

Sally shook her head.

"Good. We need all cell phones on the table *right* now." The twins reached into their hip pockets and complied. Sally said that hers was on the sink in the kitchen.

"Get it," the big man ordered. He pointed his handgun at Tanner, who was still dazed, but able to sit up on the floor where he'd landed. "Galahad, ya got a cell-phone?"

Tanner nodded his head, his nose aching badly but only dribbling slightly now. He dug out his phone, and Sally put it on the table for him.

"Landlines are where?"

"They aren't connected," Sally, who had almost pulled herself together, explained in a voice just a tiny bit higher-pitched than normal. "No one has lived here for years. We're only here for our traditional Christmas vacation." She figured since the intruders were masked the family's lives weren't endangered if they cooperated.

"Okay," the spokesman continued, "all wallets, purses, and jewelry on the table."

After a minute, everyone had complied, Sinead and Sally getting their purses from where they hung near the front door in the hallway.

"You bring any other valuables here into the house ... like money, other jewelry, watches, or expensive Christmas presents, stuff like that?"

Tanner and Sean handed over their watches.

After reluctantly taking off her diamond stud earrings and wedding ring, Sally slowly shook her head. "Nothing else I can think of ... except for the Christmas presents, under the tree in the living room. And they aren't really expensive stuff anyhow—just some video games, books, and kids' clothes. We planned on a week of hiking and quietly celebrating Christmas here on the mountain. Didn't bring any fancy jewelry or anything for dressing up."

"We'll look the presents over later." The leader turned to his two associates.

" Repeat, check out the house. Make sure all phone lines are dead. Jake, check those stairs, see what's down there."

"May I get ice for my husband's nose, give him some aspirin from my purse?" Sally asked. She'd been a RN when they were first married eighteen years ago, and remembered what to do to ease Tanner's immediate pain and facial swelling.

"Sure, lady, get him some aspirin and ice.... But remember I'm watching. You're much too pretty to be sporting a bullet hole. Okay?"

She nodded and went to get ice from the kitchen fridge, her purse still on the dining room table.

She was attending Tanner, when the man named Jake came back upstairs and reported. "It's kinda unfinished basement with a pair of beds down there. No doors or windows, the foundation sittin on exposed rock in places. Phone's definitely dead. Saw a big chest against the far wall, but it's empty. Lots of fookin books in a pair of bookcases, mostly paperbacks. Dint see nothin of real value, ya unnerstan—"

The small man came hustling back into the dining room, obviously excited.

"C-C-C—" He stomped, broke his stammer and said: "Come see w-what I found accidentally, Lil Anthony."

The Brothers herded the family ahead of them, following Repeat into the tiny office off from the master bedroom. He pointed at the floor between the desk and southern wall.

A throw rug was kicked over, and revealed a small floor safe.

Little Anthony forced a thin-lipped grin. "Well now," he said, staring menacingly at Sally, who was looking down at the safe with surprise written on her face. "Nothing else of value here, eh? What's the combination, lady?"

She frowned, and then shook her head. "We've never used it. Don't remember ever noticing it before. Must've been hidden by that throw rug the times we visited in the past."

"How bout it, Galahad?"

"Forgotten it was there," Tanner answered, his stuffed-up voice affected by his injured nose. "It was my grandfather who built the place. He owned the wagon line between Napa and Monticello. But he had his shipping office down in Napa on the river where they off-loaded the wagons onto barges destined for the City. I don't think anything of value was *ever* kept up here...." He paused before adding: "This safe probably hasn't been used or even opened by anyone for maybe ... thirty or more years since he died—"

"C'mon, man, do we look like *fucking* idiots?" Little Anthony snapped angrily. "Ya shitting me? Nobody *ever* curious about what was in that safe for over thirty years?"

Tanner just shrugged innocently in an apologetic manner.

"Well, maybe we can jog some memories," the leader said, looking at his smaller friend. "Anything else of value on this floor, Repeat?"

The little man shook his head.

"Okay, Jake, let's talk to Mama and Papa back there at the dining room table," Little Anthony said, his tone more than a hint ominous. Then, gesturing with his handgun, he said: "Repeat, take these two kids down and lock em in the basement for now, while we *discuss* things privately with their folks."

7.

It was getting cold in the basement. The twins had slept down there several times in the past during larger family gatherings, especially when their Uncle Mike came up.

Tonight, they stripped a blanket from each of the beds, wrapped them around their shoulders; but they were scared wide-awake, afraid almost to breathe, listening intently, and whispering. The voices above were muffled, but most of what was said was still intelligible.

It didn't sound like the thieves believed their parents about not knowing the floor safe combination. The crooks suspected their parents either knew or it had to be written down somewhere here in the adobe, and they wanted it. At first, they just bullied their parents verbally....

But as the night wore on, the twins cringed, huddling and holding each other closer, flinching as the dangerous crooks lost patience and began to get physical, a number of loud slaps echoing through the floor and across the basement. Then, it sounded like they were going to torture their dad in front of their mother.

"Okay, Repeat, get my K-bar out, saw off his little finger—"

"No, please, noooo...."`

"That was *Mom*," Sinead whispered, the blankets held tightly around their shoulders.

Sean nodded, but put a finger to his lips.

"We don't know, I swear," their mom added, between loud sobs. "You've cut him for nothing."

It was quiet for a long while, but a decision was finally made.

"Okay, Galahad, let's see if we can jog *your* memory," the leader said, his tone sharp and serious. "Strip off all your clothes *now*, lady. We're gonna play some grab-ass."

The twins held their collective breaths, not really believing the speaker's obvious intent....

"*Enough!*"

That last angry roar was from their dad.

Immediately, there followed the sounds of a major scuffle overhead, loud thumps and things being thrown around or knocked over and then a sudden—

Bang.

"Oh, man, you didn't have to shoot him."

"You dirty, evil bastard ..." That was their mother shrieking and apparently attacking the shooter.

Bang.

"They shot them both?" Sinead whispered, in a stunned, incredulous voice.

With tears in his eyes, and a horror-struck expression, Sean shuddered but placed his forefinger to his lips again. "*Shush.*"

Nothing.

It was dead quiet above them for what seemed like an eternity.

And then finally an angry exclamation: "Goddammit, Jake! We ain't ever going to get that combination, now," the leader said, obviously upset. "The kids probably doan know shit about it."

In a choked-up voice, Sean nodded and whispered to his sister: "They're both definitely *gone*."

Sinead just sat still on the edge of the bed, looking like a small child suddenly awakened and terrified of drowning in the dark, too shocked to reply, huge tears rolling slowly down her cheeks.... And then, as if grasping onto a lifeline in the dark, she shook herself and thought: *Well, they are back together now ...forever.*

"We're going to be next!"Her brother's sudden dreadful assessment shocked Sinead back to at least partial reality. "We need to get out of here, *right now*," Sean added.

Sinead glanced around, as if seeing the basement for the first time—no windows, only the one locked door, *no* other way out of this basement that she could see. "How?" she whispered hoarsely.

Both twins remained in place, shocked into inaction by the horrifying murder of their parents—

But at that moment a neon bluish-green apparition appeared in the cellar.

"What is it?" Sean said, a puzzled look on his face.

It seemed like a kind of brightly translucent hummingbird to Sinead, small, about the size of her fist.... It hovered over the chest against the far wall for only moment; then, it dropped down behind the chest and disappeared out of sight. After a few seconds, the iridescent figure re-appeared, and disappeared again, repeating the odd process two more times.

Finally, wiping her eyes again with the back of her wrist, Sinead said in a hoarse whisper: "Sean, I think it's some kind of friendly creature and wants us to follow."

Sean nodded, as the brightly colored thing disappeared again. He pulled the empty chest away from the wall, revealing the concrete foundation spanning a rocky outcropping. The figure had disappeared into an upside down V-like rocky crevice below the foundation that had been hidden by the chest. The opening looked just large enough for them both to crawl through. "But a very *smart* friendly creature delivering a wonderful Christmas present for us, eh?"

The twins, dragging their blankets behind, wiggled through the crevice under the foundation, finding themselves in a small depression under the foot-wide floorboards of the greenhouse. They pushed two of the old floorboards loose and slid them over, exposing a wide space. Then, both scrambled up into the greenhouse. They cloaked themselves again in their blankets, even though it felt a bit warmer here. But the air smelled stale. Sean led his sister over to the outside door of the greenhouse and signaled *wait*. He spit several times on the hinges, which were a bit rusty from years of non-use. Finally, with care, they both quietly leaned in and managed to force the stuck door open just enough to squeeze through.

Outside, the snowing had subsided, but the temperature had continued to drop.

It had to be below freezing.

"Let's get our bows," Sean whispered, pointing at the storage shed in the center of the turnaround. Glancing back at the house and seeing no one watching out the glass of the front door, the twins made their way quickly to the shed. Their unstrung practice bows were hung on pegs inside the unlocked shed—neither was weighted or balanced like their more expensive competition bows left down in Carlsbad and up at their uncle's place in Sacramento. There were five or six arrows in each of the two hanging quivers, but none with razor-sharp hunting tips, only thimble-like blunt metal practice tips. The practice arrows were better than nothing.

Sean said: "We need to get away, find a sheltered place to hide for three or four hours until dawn, when it will hopefully warm up. We won't make it very far in the dark in this chilling cold, wading through deep snow. Especially if our Converses get wet."

"Let's hide out in the horse shed down on the old wagon trail," Sinead suggested. "Then, maybe we can get out to Highway 121 after the sun rises, and hitch a ride."

Down at the horse shed, the twins huddled together under their two blankets, their feet remarkably dry but frozen numb, both teens much too cold to sleep, the two gunshots continuing to echo frightfully in their memories. They took off their shoes and rubbed some life into each others' feet.... And somehow they managed to weather the remaining few hours of night, shivering as much with fear as with the icy chill. They *knew* the killers would be coming for them soon.

8.

The three cohorts had found the basement empty, shortly after shooting the twin's parents. But knowing the two youngsters couldn't get far in the knee-deep snow during the freezing night, Little Anthony had suggested: "We'll wait until dawn, then track the lil shits' footprints in the snow. We'll catch up to them wearing our snowshoes. Let's get a few hours rest."

As the sun rose over Mt. George, the three easily tracked the twin's footprints down to where the youngsters had left the access road to wade through deep snow to reach the old wagon trail. It had stopped snowing sometime during the night, but was freezing cold.

The killers, who had abandoned their turbans and masks, paused on the wagon trail, Little Anthony pointing down at the old horse shed. "The lil shits are holed up down there. See where their fucking tracks are leading?"

They walked several hundred yards closer, until they were easily within shouting distance. Little Anthony signaled for the trio to stop. Then, he yelled: "Come out you two. We ain't gonna hurt you if you give up. We just wanta ask you a few questions. Then you can go back up the mountain to the warm house, where we left your folks tied up. They're really worried about you."

9.

The twins had heard the killers coming before the leader shouted out. Sean shook his head emphatically when the man said that they wouldn't be hurt. "They won't let us off this mountain alive, Sinead," he whispered, his lips blue with the cold. "Our folks aren't tied up at the house, they're *gone*. And now we've seen the killers' bare faces through the cracks in the shed wall, and know their first names."

Sinead nodded, trying to stomp feeling into her still chilled feet. She was so tired.

10.

That's when the luminescent creature appeared again just beyond the blackberry bushes below the capped spring.

Repeat saw it first and shouted: "L-L-Look! It must be Tinkerbell!" Then he began to run awkwardly in his snowshoes toward the hovering translucent apparition.

Suddenly, he disappeared, falling into the capped spring depression. He didn't come up. The brothers ran to the edge of the hole and looked down.

"*Jesus,*" Jake said, careful not to fall in and join his friend, who was *not* moving, his headed twisted slightly to the side, his forehead and face completely covered with blood. He looked up, but the iridescent creature had disappeared. "What the fook was that thing?"

"Who knows," Little Anthony said, pulling his brother back. "Repeat is history, man. Leave his ass."

They stepped back from the pit and glared down at the horse shed.

They both jacked rounds into the chambers of their automatics.

11.

The frozen, frightened twins watched the accident play out through the wall cracks, the two killers standing still now at the edge of the capped spring, looking mean-spirited and menacing....

Finally, Sean seemed to come to life, strung his bow and, even with frozen hands, notched an arrow. "Dad said that his Grandpa Harry claimed we came from Gaelic warrior stock, Sinead. We can't just wait here to be shot to death by these two ruthless assholes. It's time for us to stand up and fight back!"

Jacked up on adrenaline, Sean stepped to the shed doorway and let an arrow fly. But he was too amped up and his fingers too numb with cold. He missed, the arrow flying over the heads of the two killers. But they were surprised and ducked defensively, without getting off a return gunshot.

Sinead had been blowing her steamy breath on her fingers, and stepped into the doorway, a hard, brittle glint in her blue eyes. Unconcerned about being fully exposed, she took careful aim, and let fly an arrow.

It hit Jake in the upper thigh.

The big man howled and reacted instinctively, breaking the arrow off and saying: "I'm hit, Anthony, I'm hit!" He winced with pain and gasped: "The lil shits shot me with a fookin arrow!"

Little Anthony fired off a quick shot to make the dangerous archers duck back into the shed. Then he assessed the damage to his brother. "You're bleedin, man ... but it doan look too deep. Here's my snot rag. Tie it tight round your leg. We need to get you off this mountain. Can ya walk?"

After pressing the handkerchief hard for a few moments and then tying it against the broken off arrow wound, Jake tried putting weight on his injured thigh. Painfully, he successfully shuffled forward a few steps and stopped. He gritted his teeth and mumbled: "Okay, it's bleedin and hurts big time, ya unnerstan. But maybe we can make it to the truck."

Little Anthony faced to the south, the old wagon trail covered with snow but visible in some windblown places. "Okay, the pickup isn't too far off in that direction. C'mon, man."

Jake limped along behind his brother, leaving a trail of crimson spots in the wake of his snowshoe prints.

12.

Encouraged by the killers' sudden departure, Sean said with a grim edge of enthusiasm in his voice: "Let's follow them!"

"Yeah, after what they've done, we can't let *them* get away," Sinead said, her tone even more hard-edged than her brother's.

The two freshly invigorated archers were only fifty or so yards behind the fleeing killers, although they couldn't see them clearly because big snowflakes had begun to fall again, quickly covering up the men's snowshoe prints. But the wounded one left a trail, visible just under the layer of new fallen snow ... tiny scarlet flowers.

The twins waded through the snow, tracking their prey.

13.

The Arthur brothers stopped to catch their breath, Little Anthony worriedly glancing back. He saw the telltale red spots, disappearing back into the snowfall. "I think those two kids are probably stalking us, Jake. They're dangerous with those fucking bows."

The wounded brother glanced down and frowned at the red drops visible even under the new fallen snow, and nodded.

"Can you make it to the pickup by yourself?" Little Anthony asked. He pointed up into a nearby thick cluster of low-growth madrone trees. "I'll hide up there and ambush their country asses."

Jake nodded, and then with pained look of resignation on his features, he shuffled off along the trail southerly ... leaving larger, fresh bloody drops in his wake.

14.

Even without snowshoes the twins were making good time, the new snowfall not too deep on this section of the windblown trail, which ran mostly along solid bedrock.

As they approached a section winding by a steep forested slope ahead, they slowed, and finally stopped. The luminescent apparition had appeared again, hovering over a nearby cluster of ghostly trees, just barely visible through the continuing snowfall.

Sinead said: "Our *friend* is signaling something to us, Sean."

He nodded, searching the ground sloping up to the trees, and finally spotted several snowshoe tracks not completely covered yet. He whispered back: "One of the killers is hiding up there in that madrone clump."

Sinead nodded. The strange hummingbird had delivered a third Christmas present to the twins.

"I'll drop back completely out of sight, and then circle around behind him. In five minutes you make some noise down here, and draw his full attention."

Sean came down slope behind the gunman, glancing toward the wagon trail, Sinead not visible through the heavy snowfall—

"Hey, Sean, catch up," his sister shouted.

The killer stood, lifted his automatic out front like a short dowsing rod, and began to move slowly downhill to get a better shooting view.

Sean blew steamy breath onto his cold fingers for a moment, notched, and then let fly an arrow, hitting the man high in the middle of his upper back.

"*Ugh*," the killer grunted, but stayed upright, jerked around, and fired off a shot wildly.

Sean notched another arrow, aimed carefully, and shot the killer in the left side of his chest. A heart shot.

The man tumbled face down into the snow, just before Sinead appeared with a notched arrow ready in her bow. "You got him,

Sean! Good!"

"Let's get the other wounded one," Sean said with fierce determination, leading his sister back down to the wagon trail, where they saw the blood stains leading off south—

Boom.

The loud blast echoed around the startled teens.

Sean reached up to his left ear lobe, feeling as if he'd been stung by a wasp.

Looking back on the trail, about fifty feet away they saw the little man. He wasn't dead, but his face was dark scarlet with dried blood. He'd fired off a shotgun round, most of the pellets flying harmlessly over the twins' heads, but one stray nicked the tip of Sean's ear lobe. The killer jacked another shell into the chamber of his sawed-off shotgun, and sighted at the pair—

Thunk.

The small man suddenly straightened up and shuddered violently, his eyes wide and shocked ... the tip of a sharp hunting arrowhead was poking out of his throat.

Just visible a few feet back on the trail was Uncle Mike, notching another hunting arrow. But the little man had tumbled forward face-first into the snow. And he wasn't moving.

Uncle Mike picked up the shotgun and hurried up to the twins. "I saw what happened to your folks up at the house. So sorry—"

He stopped as the words caught in his throat. He brushed at his eyes, sucked in a breath, and in a hoarser voice, said: "Then I tracked the snowshoe prints down to here...." He paused to catch his breath. "You're hit," he added, finally noticing Sean's left ear.

Sean nodded, wiping blood from his ear lobe and said: "Not bad."

Sinead gently patted his wound with the tip of her blanket cloak. "I think it's okay," she said. "Let's get the last one, Uncle Mike. He's wounded and leaking blood big time." She pointed south along the wagon trail.

"You okay to follow, Sean?" Uncle Mike asked.

Sean grinned wryly and said: "My ear's so numb from the cold, I can't feel a thing. Let's get him."

The three tracked the trail of snowshoe footprints and covered red flowers.

Finally, they spotted a Dodge Ram pickup parked ahead with a driver.

Cautiously, the twins spread out beyond either side of the trail, all three moving forward, alert for any aggressive movements.

Nothing.

They moved a few steps closer.

The wounded big man was slumped forward over the steering wheel.... Alive, but out cold. He'd apparently fainted from the loss of blood.

They disarmed the unconscious killer, tied his wrists together with plastic cuffs that they'd found in the big man's backpack.

The terrible Christmas nightmare had finally ended for the twins.

Epilogue

The translucent hummingbird appeared over a spot just north of the vacant horse shed. Then, it separated into hundreds of tiny dots, which hovered for a moment ... then gently floated down to earth like luminescent greenish-blue snowflakes.

I SAW SANTA

Steve Rasnic Tem

ommy was eight years old when he first saw Santa in the flesh. Not some bloodless department store Santa, but the real Santa who came through the chimney and ate whatever you left out there for him to eat and left whatever he felt like leaving you.

Tommy had a habit of getting up most nights and wandering through the house. He was a little clumsy and he was always running into things, and afraid his parents would hear him and lose their minds. That was a funny expression but he knew it was true. He'd seen them do exactly that—get so mad their faces changed until he didn't recognize them anymore and then they'd do things, stomp around and break his toys and hit him and stuff. Tommy was big for his age but he wasn't very strong. He got hurt easily. But at least he didn't complain about it. He kept his mouth shut when he got hurt.

Christmas Eve when Tommy was eight years old he couldn't sleep. He lay in bed for a couple of hours just staring at the ceiling and listening to the house. They had an old house that made a lot of noise: pops and cracks and little stepping sounds like mice or cockroaches moving across the kitchen floor or maybe even little men—who could know for sure? When his mom and dad were

141

asleep and it was quiet enough he heard those little steps almost every night.

He got up that Christmas Eve and walked down the hall. He was really careful when he crept past his mom and dad's bedroom. He could hear them snoring—his mom sounding like she couldn't breathe, like someone was putting a hand over her mouth and then taking it away over and over again—she gasped like she was dying— his dad snarling and snorting like he was furious. Sometimes his dad talked in his sleep, and although Tommy couldn't understand the words he knew they were angry words.

His mom's fat black cat Mimi passed him in the hall. Mimi was his mom's cat because she was mean and scratched everybody else. His mom said it was because she was the only one who fed the damn thing and if some people would only do their share of the work then maybe that cat would like them too. Tommy tried to do his chores right but his mom said she might as well do them herself than let him screw things up again. Tommy didn't think the cat would like him even if he did feed her every once in awhile.

Tommy made it all the way downstairs to the living room without waking them up. He was proud of himself. Some day he would be the very best in the whole world at sneaking around. He just had to keep practicing.

Tommy pulled out his little red flashlight and let it shine on the floor and at the living room furniture and finally at the Christmas tree in the corner, dark now with its lights out. Tommy thought the tree was pretty special when they had the decorations on and everything all lit up. It didn't look that special now, all skinny and dark. Some of the ornaments lay scattered on the floor—Mimi liked to pull them off. He turned his flashlight off and on real fast a few times hoping that would make the tree special again but it didn't.

Tommy crept closer and shined his flashlight on the presents lying under the tree. There were new ones with his name on them, and they all said they were from Santa. But they were wrapped in the Christmas paper his mom bought at the grocery store last week. He'd asked her about that before. She told him Santa might bring the presents, but she sure as hell had to wrap them.

Tommy could tell he didn't get anything he'd wanted. None of the packages were shaped like a football or a basketball or any other kind of ball. That was all he'd asked for. He'd learned not to ask for much so that there would be less disappointment when he didn't get it. He picked up each wrapped package and shook it and was pretty sure they were all clothes. Well, he always needed clothes—he outgrew everything so fast. They were always telling him how much money he cost them. But he'd been hoping for something a little fun this year.

He heard a noise like a knock or a thump so he ducked behind the couch and put his ear against the floor. He figured he could hear someone coming from anywhere in the house that way. Then he heard steps across the floor, and then there was this thrumming inside his head like some kind of engine noise. He opened his eyes. It was Mimi, staring at him with her eyes wide. He waited for her to claw him but she didn't. Maybe she was in a rare good mood. Tommy put his head back down and closed his eyes, and eventually he went to sleep.

He woke up again and it was still dark, still the middle of the night. His ears were ringing like when he had a head cold, like someone was holding him underwater. He crawled on his hands and knees to the edge of the couch and looked around.

The Christmas tree lights were slowly blinking to life, a soft twinkling at first, then brighter and brighter, as if they were pulling in more and more electricity. A few of them become so bright Tommy was sure they were going to catch on fire.

The fireplace bricks began to shift and crumble. The floor was trembling. Tommy raised his hands, sure the bricks were going to fly across the room. Then something happened to the air, and he could feel this heavy pressure that stopped up his ears and made his face ache. A large red face suddenly appeared in the brick, like his dad's face when he'd been drinking too much. The face was pushing its way out of the brick, and then a red stocking cap appeared, popping out of the widening cracks, and there was Santa's bushy white beard moving around as if it were full of bugs. Then the rest of the body squeezed out of the bricks and Santa shook himself off. And when he shook he stank like a barn full of cows.

It was Santa all right, but looking nothing like any of the pictures Tommy had ever seen. Santa was taller than the Christmas tree and as wide as two refrigerators. His big, floppy face stretched out with a grin from one ear to the other. He yawned hugely and Tommy could smell his terrible breath and see his mouthful of rotting teeth. Santa's skin had gotten even redder, as red as a tomato. Tommy held his breath waiting for Santa's head to explode.

Santa looked around the room, frowning. "Where's my treat?" Tommy was afraid his mom and dad would hear and come downstairs. But maybe that was the least of his problems.

Then Santa stared right at Tommy. "Boy, come out of there! I *need* my treat! I've come a *long* way and I'm feeling a little light-headed."

Tommy crawled out from behind the couch and shakily stood up. "I guess there isn't one. I guess they didn't think you were coming."

"I see. Your mom and dad, *stingy* are they?"

"No, no. They're *nice* people, Santa. But they can't afford the moon, you know?"

"Is that what your daddy says, boy? Is he always talking about how he can't afford the moon, whatever you ask for? Well, I know the type."

His mom's cat walked between them then. Santa looked down at it and grinned. "What's the cat's name, boy?"

"M-m-mimi, Sir."

"Mimi, hmmm. Sounds *yummy*."

"My mom keeps cookies hidden in a drawer!" Tommy said quickly. "I'm not supposed to know, but I saw her put them there! I can get them for you—there's a whole bunch!"

"Well, don't just stand there! My tummy's growling!" Santa said. And it *was*. His belly sounded as if there were a bunch of fighting dogs inside.

Tommy ran into the dining room and pulled three bags of cookies from underneath a folded tablecloth in one of the sideboard drawers. When he came back Santa swept them from his arms and stuffed them down his throat bags and all. Tommy could see a huge lump move down Santa's throat until it disappeared. "Got anything else?"

"Wasn't—wasn't that *enough*?" Tommy started to back away, wondering if he could outrun Santa's long legs.

"Hmmm." Santa scratched his beard. A rat fell out of it and ran off into the dining room. Tommy could hear Mimi cry out as she began the chase. "Maybe so. I pretty much ate my fill at the Gibson house. You know the Gibsons?"

"I go to school with their son. Felix."

"Nice boy. *Very* nice. Well, maybe I've eaten enough for one night." He frowned at Tommy then, his eyes looking dark and ferocious. "You can't tell anyone about this, you hear? It's bad luck, catching Santa in the act."

Tommy nodded. "I won't, Santa."

"Good boy. Now good luck ..." He scanned the floor with all its dust, ash, and rubble. "With all this." He turned toward the chimney.

"Bye, Santa," Tommy said.

"Wait!" Santa turned back around. "Almost forgot." He pounded himself on the chest a couple of times and opened his mouth, making a deep coughing sound.

Tommy stepped back. A glistening reddish-brown football flew out of Santa's mouth, which Tommy miraculously caught. It was soaking wet and slimy, a little stinky, but it appeared to be brand new.

Santa wiped the drool off his mouth and said, "You might want to hide that, by the way, to avoid any embarrassing questions." He backed into the fireplace and started to fade into it. "Next year, don't be afraid to ask for more. As long as you remember them treats." And then he was gone.

§

Tommy started to sweep up some of the dust but of course there was no way he could fix all the broken bricks around the fireplace so he finally gave up and just went to bed. The next morning he woke up to the sounds of his dad yelling and cursing and stomping around. He went downstairs to face whatever his parents wanted to do to him.

"I know you did this—I just don't know *how* you did this," his dad said quietly, staring at him. When Tommy's dad used his soft voice like that he was even scarier. Tommy wondered if he ran out the door right then if his dad could catch him. The old man was drinking already, so maybe not.

"That boy couldn't break those bricks—he's not strong enough. You've seen him try to lift things—he's *useless*." His mom patted his dad's arm as she said this. Of course she wasn't defending Tommy—she just didn't want his dad to go on a rampage and *completely* ruin the holiday.

That all changed later that day when she discovered that the cookies were missing. Tommy went to bed without Christmas dinner, with a promise that next year he was getting nothing at all. Of course he knew his parents wouldn't remember that long, and underneath his bed he still had that bright and shiny new football.

§

For Christmas of his ninth year Tommy asked for a chemistry set. His mom and dad looked at him as if he were crazy. "There's no way!" his dad said.

"But if *Santa* brings it, can I keep it?"

His mom and dad looked at each other. His mother shrugged. His dad smiled grimly. "Sure, kid. If Santa is stupid enough to bring you something you'll blow yourself up with, sure, you can keep the damn thing."

Late Christmas Eve Tommy snuck down to the living room with a giant bag of goodies he'd been hoarding for months: licorice sticks and candy corn and apples and oranges and stale Easter Peeps, a giant bag of candy saved from Halloween, and two full jars of peanut butter and jam.

Mimi, older and still fat and still annoying kept trying to grab the treats and he had to push her away with his foot. Once she dug her claws deep into his knee and he had to bite his lip to keep from screaming. He spent some time arranging the treats in front of the fireplace (completely repaired by his dad, although several of the bricks were a different shade of red and had been put in crookedly) so that Santa would see them as soon as he appeared.

Tommy was almost finished when he felt that ringing in his ears, and then a pressure so strong it made him drop to the floor. He closed his eyes against the pain and several hard and heavy things fell on his back. He started crawling on his hands and knees as fast as he could to get away.

He bumped into something cool and smooth and he opened his eyes. It was massive, black, and shiny. Tommy leaned back a little. It was a giant boot. Looking up he saw the colossal swollen head nodding toward him, the burning black eyes and lively beard, the cheeks glowing purple. Santa grinned a shark's grin—his teeth were several inches long and came down to needle-like points.

"You're bigger," Santa said. "Too many burgers? Or is it ice cream?" Tom scrambled to his feet and backed away. Santa was so wide he hid the fireplace from view, but when he bent down and began gobbling up his treats Tommy could see that the fireplace was almost completely destroyed. One of Santa's boots crushed part of the Christmas tree, which hadn't been all that big in the first place.

Santa's oversize head wobbled like one of those carnival bobble heads as he looked around the room. "You still have that football I gave you last year?"

"Y-yes," Tommy replied. "I only play with it with my friends at the playground. M-mom and Dad, they still don't know I h-have it."

"Oh, *you* have friends?" Santa puffed out his huge blubbery lips like he didn't believe him.

"That's mean, Santa."

"Just kidding!" Santa boomed. "Don't be so *serious*!" He laughed, his belly shaking like a bowl full of—*No*, Tommy thought. Santa's belly moved in massive waves that knocked half of the living room furniture over. Tommy was glad his mom and dad had been drinking so heavily that night. Still, he wondered what might happen if they woke up and saw Santa like this. The idea of seeing their terrified faces thrilled him. "But is this *all* the treats you have? I'm *starving*! Can't you see how I'm *wasting* away?"

That stupid cat Mimi walked between them then, and before Tommy could say anything else Santa stretched out an enormous black-gloved hand and scooped the cat up and dropped her into his gaping mouth. Santa chewed some, grinding his teeth so loudly it drowned out the cat's screeches, and then he pounded his chest hard as he swallowed.

Tommy started to cry, wondering if Santa was going to eat him next.

"Hush, boy. Are you saying you *liked* that cat? Tell the truth—I know you didn't!" Tommy shook his head. "No—that's what I thought. I'm satisfied now, thanks for asking. I just needed a little protein, you know? Protein builds muscle. You need more protein, boy!"

Tommy nodded dumbly. How was he going to explain the missing cat? He looked around at the devastation. How was he going to explain *any* of this?

Santa put a finger to his nose with a drunken-looking lop-sided grin. After a minute or two with nothing happening he sighed and shook his head. Then he turned and disappeared into the gigantic hole where the fireplace used to be.

Tommy woke up the next morning to a lot of rage and anger, but much to his surprise none of it was directed at him. He came downstairs to see his dad screaming on the phone at someone from the insurance company. More of the wall behind the fireplace had collapsed, leaving a clear view to the outside. He could see his mom through the hole, out in the yard calling for Mimi. Dust and bricks were everywhere. Whatever was left of the Christmas tree lay on its side, covered in rubble.

"I don't know *when* it happened! We were *asleep*, dammit! How should *I* know? It's been a rough holiday—we needed our sleep I guess. I *work* for a living! I just want you to do your *job* and get out here!" His dad slammed down the phone. He looked at Tommy, frowning. "Somebody drove into the side of the house last night. You didn't hear anything?"

Tommy shook his head. "Not a peep."

"Well, neither did we. And that damn *cat* ran away."

His mother came stumbling back inside through the hole in the wall. Tommy thought to tell her how dangerous that was, but figured he'd better keep his mouth shut. Her face was wet from crying, which surprised him. He never thought she might actually love that cat. "Well, she's gone for good!" she cried. "Or else they took her."

"Who the hell would want ..." his father began, but then the terrible look on his mom's face stopped all conversation.

It wasn't until they were cleaning up that afternoon that his dad found the package in the corner, undamaged. "What the hell is *this*!" He held up a giant brightly-colored box. *Junior Mad Scientist's Chemistry Set!* was emblazoned in neon green lettering across the front of the box.

"It looks like Santa brought me that chemistry set I asked for," Tommy said, beaming.

His dad glanced at the kitchen where his mother was fixing dinner. "I'll kill her," he muttered.

"You *said* I could keep it if *Santa* brought it," Tommy said, not quite able to get rid of his smile.

His dad put down the box and went upstairs for the rest of the day.

§

Tommy spent most of the next year gathering together everything he could think of that a monstrous and unpredictable Santa might eat. His parents never came into his room anymore so he had no worries about them finding anything.

Some of these Santa treats were canned goods he'd pilfered from the kitchen, taken one can at a time and not very often so his mother didn't suspect anything. Now and then he'd take one of his dad's beers, and once a bottle of whiskey hidden in some towels. That caused a big fight between his mom and dad but they were always fighting anyway so he didn't feel too guilty about it. They were still fighting over who gave him that chemistry set—each calling the other a liar.

By the time his tenth Christmas rolled around Tommy had ample food to feed an army of regular Santas, and he hoped it would somehow satisfy this monster Santa once and for all. He had a dozen or more boxes of canned food, huge stacks of stale bread loaves, sacks full of candies and spoiled fruit, and a load of stuff no normal person would eat—rotten fish heads and a dead squirrel and his old marble collection.

His dad lost his job early in the year and was home most of the time drinking. His mom worked long hours for a house cleaning company and was so tired and disgusted when she got home she didn't clean their own house anymore. Most nights they had pizza or Tommy heated up his own Ramen noodle soup. He didn't know how his dad survived—Tommy hardly ever saw him eat.

But he made a long Christmas list anyway. What did it matter? Santa was the one who brought the good presents. Tommy asked for a big kid's bike, video game console, a weight lifting set, skateboard, a box of toy soldiers, a bunch of adventure books, and so many other things he couldn't remember them all. His parents took one look at his list and didn't say a word. Later he found it crumpled up in the trash.

On Christmas Eve his parents went to bed early leaving Tommy by himself. They never got around to decorating the tree so Tommy made ornaments out of construction paper, tape and glue, and hung them from the sparse branches.

It took a long time to haul all of Santa's food downstairs. At least there weren't any presents around taking up space. If his parents had bought him anything he certainly hadn't seen evidence of it.

The fireplace had been rebuilt with the insurance money. The investigator couldn't understand why there were no tire tracks out in the yard, but couldn't come up with any other rational explanation for the damage. The company paid, and then cancelled their home insurance. His dad had railed about it all year long.

Tommy didn't know what they'd do if the fireplace was destroyed again. Maybe they'd have to move. Not such a bad thing— maybe Santa wouldn't be able to find them at a new address.

As soon as the last bit of food was in place Tommy felt a rumbling deep beneath his feet, then the house began to shake, mildly at first but increasing until pictures were falling off the walls. He felt a sudden blast of heat behind him and turned around to discover a fire in the new fireplace.

He studied the flames. They came to multiple points like a mouthful of glowing red teeth. Then he noticed the huge deep-set eyes at the back of the fireplace.

The interior of the fireplace was pushing out toward him, expanding, becoming this fierce red face, dragging flaming whiskers and hair and sideburns behind it, and an elongated body that might have been a giant snake's, but which Tommy now realized looked more like a train. It poured its way down the chimney and out of the fireplace and across the living room.

A double door slid open in the side of the train and a naked red elf appeared, throwing a shiny new bicycle out into the room. Tommy grabbed it and immediately climbed on. It was incredible. He drove it into the dining room and rode it around the table a few times as the Santa train roared through the living room consuming everything in sight—not only the food, but the tree and all the furniture disappearing into its flaming maw. "Ho ho ho!" tooted the Santa horn.

Tommy stopped and looked into Santa's train engine face. "Is this all I get?"

The Santa train roared, flames shooting out of its mouth. "Is that all *you get*? What else do you have to *feed* me?"

Tommy thought for a second. "Well I guess there's some food in the refrigerator. Leftovers mostly, my mom doesn't ..."

Before he could finish the Santa train was locomoting into the kitchen, narrowing itself to get through the door. There was an explosive racket of metal screeches and heavy things being pushed around, cabinets scraped from walls and their contents crashing to the hard linoleum floor.

All this made Tommy very nervous so he rode his new bike around the table a few more times. It was all he could think of to do.

"Tommy?" It was his mother's voice. He looked back into the living room and his parents were standing there in their pajamas and robes. It surprised him how colorless they looked. Compared to everything else they looked like they had no color at all. They were like black and white people who had accidentally wandered into a color movie.

Tommy rode his bike around the table as fast as he could. "See what Santa brought me? Santa brought me a new bike!"

The Santa train came roaring out of the kitchen then with its mouth and whiskers and eyebrows on fire. It ran right over his mom and dad before it came to a stop.

"So what *else* do you want?" the Santa train bellowed.

"I can't decide I can't decide!" Tommy cried, still racing his bike around the table.

The train door slid open again and three naked red elves waved. They appeared to be surrounded by row after row of shelves overflowing with toys, but it was hard to tell exactly what was on the shelves, or how far they extended. But just the glimpse made Tommy's mouth go dry with excitement. "Then come inside come inside!" the elves cried in unison.

And after once more around the table that's exactly what Tommy did, the door snapping shut so quickly behind him it severed his bike in two.

SILENT NIGHT

Richard Chizmar

he man sat in his car parked alongside the cemetery and finished his cigarette. The engine was off and the driver's window was down. It was raining, not too hard, not too soft, a steady rain that drummed the man a lonely lullaby on the roof of his car and soaked his left elbow, which was propped out the window.

He reached over with a gloved hand and dropped the butt into an empty water bottle sitting on the passenger seat next to him. He did this by feel, never once taking his eyes off the cemetery grounds. He scanned from left to right, and back again.

The cemetery had been crowded earlier—always was this time of year—but now the grounds were nearly abandoned thanks to the late hour and the cold and rain. His eyes touched an elderly man a few hundred yards to his right. The old man had been there for the better part of an hour, standing still and rigid, staring down at a grave marker, lost in thought and memory. A middle-aged couple knelt on the wet ground directly in front of the man's car, maybe a hundred yards out. Had they lost a child, the man wondered? Or were they mourning a mother or father or both? The man thought it could have been all three. The way this world works.

153

The old-timer left first, weaving his way surprisingly fast between the headstones to a faded red pick-up. The truck started with a backfire that sounded too much like a gunshot and slunk away into the twilight. The man watched the taillights fade to tiny red sparks and imagined a dinner table set for one awaiting the old man at home and wished he hadn't.

Five minutes later, the middle-aged man helped the middle-aged woman to her feet and, with wet knees, they walked hand-in-hand to a gray SUV parked at the opposite end of the road. The middle-aged woman never looked up, but the middle-aged man did. Just before he opened his car door and got inside, he glanced back at the man and nodded.

The man remained perfectly still in his car. He didn't return the nod and he didn't lift a hand to wave. He cast his eyes downward for a moment out of habit, an old trick, but he knew it wasn't necessary. He was being paranoid again. He gauged the distance at sixty yards and it was raining and his wipers weren't on. The middle-aged man was merely nodding at a dark shape behind blurry glass; a polite acknowledgement that he and the man sitting alone in his car both belonged to the same somber fraternity. A moment of kindness shared, and nothing else.

The man watched the middle-aged couple drive away and fought the urge to light up another cigarette. He scanned the cemetery grounds, left to right and back again, waited five more minutes to be sure, and then he got out of the car.

§

Let's pretend, for just a moment, that Forest Hills Memorial Gardens employs a night watchman. And let's further pretend that, at 6:19 p.m. on December 24, this watchman is lurking in the dark shadows just inside the treeline of gnarly old pines that marks the cemetery's northern most property line, perhaps smoking a cigar (which is strictly prohibited by employee rules) or perhaps just trying to keep dry in the rain.

If this scenario is indeed accepted as fact instead of fiction, then this is what our stealthy night watchman might witness at that particular time on that particular night:

A single man exits the lone car that remains parked on cemetery property, a dark sedan with rental license plates. The man is of medium height but broad in his chest and shoulders. He looks around, like he's making sure he's alone, straightens his jacket, lowers his winter hat, and despite walking with a slight limp, he makes his way quickly and confidently to a nearby gravesite. The man's eyes never stop moving beneath that winter hat, and the path he takes is precise and direct. The man has been here before.

Once he reaches his destination, the man bends down and places a single red rose—our night watchman has wickedly sharp eyesight—at the base of a headstone, where it joins several other much fancier flower arrangements and a plastic Santa decoration with a candle inside, its flame long since drenched by the falling December rain. The man traces a finger along the names engraved on the marker, and now the watchman notices that he is wearing gloves on both of his hands, and then he catches a glimpse of something much more interesting: a flash of dark gunmetal at the back of the man's waistband.

The man doesn't linger. He quickly stands up, readjusts his jacket and once again surveys the cemetery, slower this time, as if he somehow senses the watchman's presence there in the trees, and then he heads back to his car without a backward glance.

Within a heartbeat of closing his car door, the man starts the engine and speeds out of the cemetery. Headlights off and nary a tapping of brake lights. A dark shadow swallowed by the night and the approaching storm.

High in the towering pines, the rain changes over to snow and the wind picks up, whispering its secrets.

But the cemetery is deserted now and there is no one left to hear.

The man is gone, and, of course, our night watchman never existed.

§

"Are you Santa Claus?"

The man stopped in mid-step, one foot in the kitchen, one

foot still in the family room, staring over his shoulder at the little boy standing in the glow of the Christmas tree lights. The boy was wearing red-and-white pajamas and blinking sleep from his eyes. The man slowly removed his hand from the gun in his waistband, where it had instinctually moved to at the sound of the boy's voice, turned around, and lifted a finger to his lips. *Sshhh.*

The little boy—nine years old and named Peter, the man knew—wrinkled his nose in confusion, but stayed quiet.

The man slowly stepped back into the family room. His hands held out in front of him. "It's okay," he whispered. "I was just on my way out."

The little boy moved closer, unafraid, and whispered right back: "If you're not Santa, then who are you?"

The man didn't know what to say, so he just stood there, memorizing every inch of the little boy. He had entered the house twenty minutes earlier through the basement door. It had been too easy; he hadn't even needed to use his special tools. He'd crept up the carpeted stairs, silent as a house cat, and eased his way into a dark kitchen, and then the family room, where he'd found a Christmas tree tucked into the corner by the fireplace with dozens of wrapped presents waiting beneath it. The man had stood there in the quiet darkness for a long time, taking it all in. The decorations on the tree, many of which he recognized. The framed pictures on the mantel, several featuring the man's younger, smiling face. He stared at the paintings on the wall, the knickknacks on the shelves, the furniture, even the curtains. This was the man's first—and most likely last—time inside the new house, and he wanted to soak up everything he could into his memory banks ... to remember later.

Somehow he had missed the little boy, who'd probably snuck downstairs after his mother had fallen asleep and curled up on the sofa beneath a blanket waiting for Santa. Some agent he was ...

"You know what? You look a lot like my Uncle Bobby," the little boy whispered, his cute little nose all wrinkled up again. "Only his hair is a lot longer than yours."

The man felt his eyes grow wet and fought it back. His pulse quickened. There was so much he wanted to say. So much he needed to say.

But he knew he couldn't.

The letter and box of money he had placed under the tree would have to be enough.

The man reached out and rested a shaky, gloved hand on the boy's small shoulder.

"Give your mom and Uncle Bobby a hug for me. I bet they're awesome folks." The man bent down and kissed the top of the boy's head—and that was when he smelled her on the little boy. His wife. Even after all those years.

Inhaling deeply, voice shaking now, the man said, "I left you all something under the tree."

The little boy's eyes flashed wide and, with a smile, he looked back at the Christmas tree. "What did you leave us?" he asked.

But when he turned back around, the man was gone.

§

Even with the drifting snow and occasional tears blurring his vision, the man traveled back roads to the airport, careful to make certain no one was following him. He hoped he was just being paranoid, but he couldn't be sure. It had been a quiet fifteen months since they had almost found him in Mexico. Two years before that, they had somehow tracked him to the coast of Venezuela, and it was only with God's good grace that he'd remained a free man. They would never stop looking, and he would never stop running. He knew too much; had seen and done too much.

The plows hadn't touched most of the back roads, so the going was slow. That was okay with the man. The airport was only twenty-seven miles away, and he had almost three hours to return the rental car and make his gate for the return flight overseas. Better safe than sorry, he thought, although even if a policeman found him stuck on the side of the road in a ditch, he should be fine. His rental papers were in order, and he carried a legal driver's license, credit cards, Social Security card and everything else he needed to appear a normal, law-abiding U.S. citizen. If, for any reason, the cop decided to search his rental car, then that would be another story. The man would be forced to resort to other options.

With that thought in mind, the man glanced in the rearview mirror and dropped his speed another five miles per hour. He turned the windshield wipers up a notch. The man knew he would have to be at his most vigilant at the airport. These days, they watched the international flights with special attention, especially around the holidays. He would dispose of his weapons once he reached the rental car return lot, but not a moment sooner.

Ten minutes later, the winding back road he was traveling on merged with MD Route 40 and soon after he passed an old-fashioned road sign that read WELCOME TO EDGEWOOD. The man looked at the sign with a sad smile.

Maybe a mile later, he slowed through an intersection beneath a blinking yellow traffic light that was dancing wildly in the whipping wind and snow. There was a strip mall bordering the right side of the road, all the stores gone dark except for a Dunkin Donuts at the far end of the building. Twin mounds of snow covered two small cars in the parking lot, probably belonging to the unfortunate workers inside.

The man tapped the brakes and steered into the parking lot, feeling his back tires slide a little in the accumulating slush. He swung around and parked facing the road, away from the Dunkin Donuts front windows, and turned off the car. His eyes had grown weary, and he knew from experience that strong coffee was the remedy. His stomach was talking to him, too. He thought maybe a couple chocolate donuts or a hot breakfast sandwich, if they served those this time of night.

The man got out of his car and watched as a snowplow loomed out of the darkness like some kind of huge, prehistoric animal, its glowing yellow eyes illuminating the swirling snow. The driver flipped him a wave from inside the warmth of his cab, and this time the man waved back. He was halfway to the front door of Dunkin Donuts when his wrist began to vibrate. Startled, the man looked down at his arm and thumbed a button on the side of his watch, silencing it.

It was midnight.

Christmas.

The man stopped in the middle of the parking lot, oblivious

to the cold and falling snow. It had been ten Christmases since he'd last held her in his arms. Ten impossibly long years. She had been pregnant with his child then—with Peter. They had been so excited that they were going to be parents. They had painted and decorated the nursery together. Shopped for outfits and baby supplies. They had been happy.

Six months later, on a routine assignment in Turkey, the man had found himself in the wrong place at the wrong time— and instead of helping him, his government had tried to solve the problem by erasing his existence. He'd been on the run ever since. Running from dangerous men trained just as he had been trained, from men he once called his brothers. They would laugh at him now, the man thought. Tired and hungry and crying, sneaking back home like a scared mouse in the forest. They had taught him better than that. They had taught him to be superhuman. Invisible. Immortal.

The man let out a deep breath and watched the vapor fill the air in front of his face. The night was hushed and serene, not even the falling snow hitting the store's front windows making a sound, and it made the man think of nights like this when he'd been just a kid, sledding down Hanson Hill long after dark with his neighborhood friends, their excited voices echoing across the snowy fields.

The man glanced down Route 40 toward the blinking yellow traffic light. Imagined driving back there and turning left, cruising two miles up Hanson Road to the house he had grown up in. It had been a happy house. Filled with board games and books and laughter. Filled with the love of his parents and his baby brother and the eternal mysteries of three older sisters.

Then he imagined turning left at the intersection, taking Mountain Road until it spilled into 22, following it for twenty minutes or so until it took him right back to the cemetery.

The cemetery ...

... where his mother and father had been buried.

... where the United States Government had claimed to bury him with full military honors.

The man stood there alone in the middle of the strip mall

parking lot, his hands beginning to shake despite his gloves, his mind betraying him with visions of empty coffins buried in frozen ground and little boys looking up at him with wide, innocent eyes, asking, *Are you Santa Claus?*

And this time he couldn't stop the tears from falling. Sloppy cold tears, equal parts shame and regret.

He should have answered him, the man thought in a panic. He should have told him, "That's right, son, I'm Santa. My red suit's in the wash ..."

Or at the very least—the truth. He owed him that much: "No, not Santa, son. I'm no one. Just a ghost."

Instead, he'd said nothing and snuck away into the night.

Out on the road, another snowplow roared by, heading in the opposite direction.

The man blinked, as if waking from a deep dream, turned around and walked back to his car. He got inside and drove away.

Away from the only home he'd ever known.

Away from everything.

"A ghost," the man whispered to himself in the darkness and drove on toward the airport.

The man wasn't tired or hungry anymore.

DECEMBER BIRTHDAY

Jeff Strand

10 Years Ago
"It's a birthday present *and* a Christmas present!" said Aunt Jenny, as Clyde opened the box and looked at his new pair of gloves.

"Thanks," said Clyde.

9 Years Ago
"Happy birthday!" said Grandma over the phone. "Are you excited about Christmas? Santa Claus is almost here! I hope you were good!"

"I was," said Clyde.

8 Years Ago
"It's a birthday present *and* a Christmas present!" said Jake. "My mom said it was okay to do it that way and you were probably used to it."

"That's fine," said Clyde.

7 Years Ago
"I can't come to your party," said Melissa. "All my relatives are in town. We're putting up the tree tonight."

"Okay," said Clyde.

6 Years Ago

"Your birthday present's in Christmas paper because it's both a birthday *and* a Christmas present," said Amy.

"How thoughtful," said Clyde.

5 Years Ago

"You're lucky, Clyde," said Mortimer. "I never get to go out caroling on my birthday!"

"It's great," said Clyde.

4 Years Ago

"Happy birthday!" said Abigail. "Here's your present! You can't open it until the 25th, though. It's a birthday *and* a Christmas present!"

"That makes sense," said Clyde.

3 Years Ago

"Oh, I'd love to go," said Henry, "but I don't know when we're going to get back from the mall. I haven't even started my Christmas shopping yet."

"No problem," said Clyde.

2 Years Ago

"Thank you," said Clyde. "I didn't even know they made a Christmas edition of Monopoly."

"Since it's a birthday *and* a Christmas present, I wanted to get you something appropriate," said Joe.

"Of course," said Clyde.

1 Year Ago

"Sorry it's just a card," said Daphne. "I'm broke around the holidays. You know how it is."

"Yes," said Clyde.

Today

"It's a birthday present *and* a Christmas present," said Uncle Mitch.

"Thank you," said Clyde, just before he reached under his

Christmas sweater, took out a revolver, and shot Uncle Mitch in the face. Blood and brain matter splattered against the tree.

Everybody screamed.

"Who else wants to give me a combination birthday/Christmas present?" Clyde demanded, waving the gun around at the other five people in the living room. "Anybody? C'mon, I know you motherfuckers have more combined gifts for me! *Who else?*"

"Just calm down," said Dad, stepping forward. "There's no reason to get upset."

Clyde pointed the gun at their elderly next-door neighbor. "Hey, Mrs. Grayson! You brought over a gift, didn't you? I see it right there on the dining room table! Nice red and green paper! I love the candy cane under the bow—very festive! How about you go get my present so we can continue the celebration, huh?"

"I don't think this is the appropriate time," said Mrs. Grayson.

"I disagree! It's party time, bitch! Go get it!"

Trembling and weeping, the old woman stood up and slowly walked into the dining room. She suddenly turned and tried to make a run for it, but her left foot twisted underneath her and she fell to the floor.

Clyde stormed into the dining room. He picked the package up by the ribbon. "Oh, look. It's to Clyde. Happy Birthday/Merry Christmas."

"I'm sorry!" said Mrs. Grayson. "Money is tight during the holi—"

Clyde threw the present to the floor, then shot her in the throat.

He waved the gun at the remaining four people. "Nobody move! My present to myself is that I get to watch her die!"

Mrs. Grayson clutched at her neck, blood spurting between her fingers. She was dead before "God Rest Ye Merry Gentlemen" had finished playing on the radio.

"Who's next?" Clyde asked.

"Please calm down," said Dad. "Please, son, you have to remember that the true spirit of Christmas is about giving, not receiving!"

"Fuck you, Dad!" Clyde shouted, shooting Dad in the stomach.

"That bullet was for Christmas *and* your birthday! How does it feel? How does it feel, Dad?"

"We never did that!" Dad insisted, as he fell to the floor. Mom let out a wail of anguish and horror.

"No, but you let it happen! You didn't protect me from the others! Betty always had a huge July celebration! She had clowns and ponies at her parties! Where were my clowns and ponies, Dad? *Where were my clowns and ponies?*"

"We're sorry!" said Mom. "It wasn't our fault! You were unplanned! We never would have done this to you on purpose! We'd just moved into our own home and we weren't used to having privacy!"

"You ruined my life!"

Mom gestured around the living room. "But, sweetheart, we're having a party for you right now!"

"Bullshit! This isn't a birthday party! These people happened to stop over!" He shot Aunt Penny between the eyes. Before she'd finished tumbling out of the recliner, he pointed the gun at the postman. "He's just here because you offered him hot cocoa!"

"There are a bunch of birthday presents for you out in my truck!" said the postman. "I was going to get them after I finished my cocoa! I'll go right out and get them!"

Clyde shot the postman in the head. He spilled the hot drink all over his lap but was too dead to feel the scalding pain.

"Please, son ..." said Dad. "Don't ... don't do this ..." He coughed up some blood, then began to sing. "*Happy birthday ... to ... you ... happy ... birth ...... day .... to ......*" His eyes glazed over and he went silent.

"*... you ...*" Mom continued. "*Happy Birthday dear Clyde, happy—*" Clyde shot her.

"I totally get where you're coming from," said the last person alive, Mr. Taylor, who lived two houses down. "My birthday isn't just in December. My birthday is on *Christmas.*"

"That must suck," said Clyde.

"Oh, God, does it ever! One year my parents just put candles in the fruitcake. Can you imagine? So I understand what you're going through. I understand why you wanted to go on a killing spree. But I am not your enemy. I'm the only one who truly knows your anguish."

"Let me see your driver's license," said Clyde.

"What?"

"I said, let me see your driver's license or some other form of identification."

"I, uh, didn't bring my wallet with me."

"What's your zodiac sign?"

"Huh? Oh, uh ..."

"You lying piece of crap," said Clyde, before he pulled the trigger. Mr. Taylor's nose exploded.

Clyde gazed at the corpses. Some would call it an extreme reaction. Some would dismiss him as a lunatic. But he'd share his message with all who would listen.

He could hear sirens in the distance. Clyde went into the kitchen, where his birthday cake rested on the counter. He lit the candles and took a deep breath.

He could be the catalyst of change for future generations. He could be a cautionary tale of the dangers of downplaying birthdays just because of their proximity to the most popular holiday of the year.

Clyde made his birthday wish and blew out the candles.

The End

Made in the USA
Monee, IL
19 January 2023

24663632R00100